Grimalkin carves the symbol of her
scissors on trees to mark her territory
or warn others away . . .

The current assassin of the Malkin clan is Grimalkin. Very fast and strong, this assassin has a code of honour and never resorts to trickery. She prefers her opponent to be a challenge. Although honourable, Grimalkin also has a dark side and is reputed to use torture. All fear the *snip-snip* of her terrible scissors.

She uses these to shear the flesh and bone of her enemies . . . Grimalkin's favourite killing tool is the long blade, and she is a skilled blacksmith who forges her own weapons.

Taken from John Gregory's notebook,
The Spook's Bestiary

THE WARDSTONE CHRONICLES

ALSO AVAILABLE

COMING SOON

Grimalkin made her first Wardstone Chronicles appearance in *The Spook's Battle* when she was sent by the Pendle witches to kill Thomas Ward.

Since then she has featured in her own short story (in the anthology *The Spook's Stories: Witches*) where we learned about her background and extreme hatred for her sworn enemy – the Fiend.

Now this deadly witch assassin has formed an alliance with Tom, the Spook and Alice. The narrative follows straight on from the end of *The Spook's Destiny*. What Grimalkin carries must be kept out of the clutches of their enemies at all costs . . .

SPOOK'S
I AM GRIMALKIN

JOSEPH DELANEY

Illustrations by David Wyatt

RED FOX

SPOOK'S: I AM GRIMALKIN
A RED FOX BOOK 978 1 849 41471 5

First published in Great Britain by Bodley Head
an imprint of Random House Children's Publishers UK
A Random House Group Company

Bodley Head edition published 2011
Red Fox edition published 2012

1 3 5 7 9 10 8 6 4 2

The Random House Group Limited supports the Forest Stewardship Council (FSC®),
the leading international forest certification organization. Our books carrying the FSC
label are printed on FSC®-certified paper. FSC is the only forest certification scheme
endorsed by the leading environmental organizations, including Greenpeace. Our paper
procurement policy can be found at www.randomhouse.co.uk/environment.

MIX
Paper from
responsible sources
FSC® C016897

Set in 10.5/16.5 Palatino by Falcon Oast Graphic Art Ltd

Red Fox Books are published by Random House Children's Publishers UK,
61–63 Uxbridge Road, London W5 5SA

www.randomhousechildrens.co.uk
www.totallyrandombooks.co.uk
www.randomhouse.co.uk

Addresses for companies within The Random House Group Limited
can be found at: www.randomhouse.co.uk/offices.htm

THE RANDOM HOUSE GROUP Limited Reg. No. 954009

A CIP catalogue record for this book is available from the British Library.

Printed and bound in Great Britain by CPI Group (UK) Ltd, Croydon, CR0 4YY

for Marie

THE HIGHEST POINT IN THE COUNTY
IS MARKED BY MYSTERY.
IT IS SAID THAT A MAN DIED THERE IN A
GREAT STORM, WHILE BINDING AN EVIL
THAT THREATENED THE WHOLE WORLD.
THEN THE ICE CAME AGAIN, AND WHEN IT
RETREATED, EVEN THE SHAPES OF THE
HILLS AND THE NAMES OF THE TOWNS
IN THE VALLEYS CHANGED.
NOW, AT THAT HIGHEST POINT ON
THE FELLS, NO TRACE REMAINS OF WHAT
WAS DONE SO LONG AGO,
BUT ITS NAME HAS ENDURED.
THEY CALL IT —

THE WARDSTONE.

CHAPTER
A LARGE GREEN BITTER APPLE

A LARGE GREEN BITTER APPLE

*Look closely at the enemy before you. Do you see his
bulging eyes and berserker fury? Do you see his hairy
chest? Can you smell his unwashed body? Keep calm.
Why be afraid? You can win. After all, he is just a
man. Learn to believe me. I am Grimalkin.*

Once I reached the centre of the wood, I swung
the heavy leather sack down from my shoulder
and placed it on the ground before me. Then I knelt
and undid the cord that sealed it – to be met by the
rank stink of what lay within. I grimaced and drew
forth what it contained, holding it up before me by its
hair, which was greasy and matted with dirt.

It was very dark beneath the trees and the moon would not rise for another hour. But my witchy eyes could see clearly despite the gloom, and I gazed upon the severed head of the Fiend, the Devil himself.

It was a terrible sight to behold. I had stitched the eyelids shut so that he could see nothing; I had stuffed his mouth with a large green bitter apple wrapped in a tangle of rose thorns so that he could not speak. My enemy had been well looked after; dealt with exactly as he deserved. Notwithstanding the stench, neither the head nor the apple had rotted; the first was due to his power, the second a result of my magic.

I spread the sack out on the ground and lowered the head onto it. Then I sat cross-legged opposite it, scrutinizing my enemy carefully.

Somehow it looked smaller now than it had appeared when freshly severed, but it was still almost twice the size of the average human head. Was it shrinking as a result of being separated from its body? I wondered. The horns that protruded from its forehead were coiled and curved like those of a ram;

the nose resembled an eagle's beak. It was a cruel face and deserved the cruelty that I had inflicted upon it in turn.

All about my body, a series of leather straps bore scabbards that held my weapons and tools. From the smallest of these I withdrew a thin sharp hook with a long handle. I thrust it into the Fiend's open mouth, pushed it deep into the green apple, and twisted and tugged. For a second there was resistance, but then I pulled the fruit out, bringing with it the tangle of rose thorns.

Relieved of the obstruction, the mouth slowly closed. I could see the broken teeth within: I had smashed them with my hammer as the Spook, Tom Ward and I had bound the Fiend. The memory of it was vivid, and I watched it again in my mind's eye.

Long had I waited for the opportunity to bind or destroy the Fiend, my greatest enemy. Even as a child I'd disliked him intensely. I observed the subtle ways in which he increasingly controlled my clan;

saw how the coven fawned over him. They spent most of each year looking forward to the Halloween sabbath, the time when he was most likely to visit. Sometimes he appeared right in the centre of their fire, and they reached forward, desperate to touch his hairy hide, oblivious to the flames that seared their bare arms.

My growing revulsion was something instinctive in me – a natural born hatred – and I knew that unless I acted, he would become a blight upon my life; a dark shadow over everything I did. He was clever, subtle and devious, often achieving his aims slowly. Above all I feared that one day, like many other witches who had once opposed him, I would finally become in thrall to him. That I could not bear and I needed to do something to make it impossible.

And I knew exactly what I had to do: there is one certain way in which a witch can ensure that he keeps his distance. It is very extreme but it means that she can be free of him for evermore. She needs to sleep with him just once, then bear his child. Thereafter –

having inspected his offspring – he may not approach her again. Not unless she wishes it.

Most of the Fiend's children prove to be abhumans, misshapen creatures of the dark with terrible strength; others are powerful witches. But a few, a very few, are born perfect human children untainted by evil. I knew I risked giving birth to a dark entity, but it seemed worth it to be rid of the Fiend.

I was fortunate indeed. Mine was a beautiful, fragile baby boy, perfect in every way.

I had never felt such intense love for another creature. To have his soft warmth against my body, so trusting, so very dependent, was wonderful – blissful beyond anything I had dreamed of; something I had never imagined or anticipated. That little child loved me, and I loved him in return; he depended upon me for life, and for the first time I was truly happy. But in this world such happiness rarely lasts.

I remember well the night mine ended. The sun had just set and it was a warm summer's evening, so I walked out into the walled garden at the rear of my cottage, cradling my child, humming to him softly to lull him to sleep. Suddenly lightning flashed overhead and I felt the ground shift beneath my feet; the air became sharp with cold. Although I had anticipated a visit from the Fiend for some time, I suddenly realized that his arrival was now imminent and my heart lurched with fear. At the same time I was glad because once he'd seen his son, I knew that he would leave and never be able to visit me again. I would be rid of him for the rest of my life.

Previously, the Fiend had always appeared to me as a handsome young man with dark curly hair, blue eyes and a mouth that often turned up at the corners with a warm, welcoming smile. But he can take on many shapes, and this time he appeared in the form that the Pendle witches refer to as 'his fearsome majesty'; it is a shape that is used to intimidate and terrify.

He materialized very near where I was standing, and his fetid breath was so close to my face that I struggled not to retch. He was large – three times my height – with the curved horns of a ram and a huge naked body covered in matted black hair. No sooner had he appeared than, with a roar of rage, he snatched my innocent baby boy and lifted him high, ready to dash him to the ground.

'Please!' I begged. 'Don't hurt him. I'll do anything, but please let him live. Take my life instead!'

The Fiend never even glanced at me. He was filled with wrath and cruelty. He smashed my child's fragile head against a rock. Then he vanished.

For a long time I was insane with grief. And then, as the long days and sleepless nights slowly passed, thoughts of revenge began to swirl within my head. Was it possible? I asked myself. Could I destroy the Fiend?

Impossible or not, that became my goal and my only reason for living.

I achieved part of that goal just one month ago. The Fiend is not destroyed, but at least he is temporarily bound. That binding was accomplished with the help of the old Spook, John Gregory, and his young apprentice, Thomas Ward. We transfixed the Fiend with silver spears, then nailed his hands and feet to the bedrock of the deep pit at Kenmare in the southwest of Ireland, where his body is now buried.

I still delight in remembering the moment of our victory. The Fiend was standing on all fours, tossing his head about like an enraged bull and roaring with pain. I stabbed the first nail into his left hand, then struck the broad head three times with the hammer, driving it right through the flesh to pin his huge hairy paw fast to the rock. However, in my eagerness to bind him I became careless, and that was the moment when I almost died.

He twisted his head, opened his mouth wide and lunged towards me as if to bite my head from my body. But I avoided those deadly jaws, then swung the hammer back hard into his face, smashing his front teeth into fragments and leaving only broken bloody stumps. Few things have given me greater satisfaction!

After that, Tom Ward wielded the Destiny Blade given to him by Cuchulain, the greatest of Ireland's dead heroes. With two deadly blows, the Spook's apprentice cut through the Fiend's neck and I carried that severed head away with me.

While body and head are apart, the Devil is bound. But his dark servants pursue me. They want to return the head to its body and pluck out the nails and silver spears so that he is free once more.

To thwart them, I keep moving. By so doing, I buy time so that the Spook and his apprentice can discover the means by which the Fiend may finally be destroyed or returned to the dark. But I cannot run for ever and my strength is finite. Besides, it is in my nature to fight, not run. This is a conflict I cannot win; there are too many of them – too many powerful denizens of the dark for even the witch assassin of the Malkin clan to overcome.

'It feels good to have you in my power!' I told the Fiend as I sat in front of him.

For a moment the severed head did not reply, but then the mouth slowly opened and a dribble of blood-flecked saliva trickled down his chin.

'Unstitch my eyes!' he bellowed, his voice a deep growl. His lips moved but the words seemed to rise up from the ground beneath the head.

'Why should I do that?' I demanded. 'If you could see, you'd tell your servants where I am. Besides, it is my pleasure to watch you suffer.'

'You can never win, witch!' he snarled, showing his broken teeth again. 'I am immortal; I can outlast even time itself. One day you will die and I will be waiting. What you have done to me I will repay a thousand times over. You cannot begin to imagine the torments that await you.'

'Listen, fool!' I told him. 'Listen well! I don't dwell on past failings, nor do I project my mind into the future more than is necessary. I am a creature of the "now" and I live in the present. And you are here in the present, trapped with me. It is you who suffer now. You are in *my* power!'

'You are strong, witch,' the Fiend said quietly, 'but something stronger and more deadly stalks you. Your days are numbered.'

Suddenly everything grew quiet and still. Our reference to 'time' had spurred him to attempt again what he had already tried but failed to do the previous time I'd lifted him out of the sack. He had the ability to slow or halt time – though being separated from his body had limited his usual powers. However, taking no chances, I rammed the thorn-wrapped apple back into his mouth, then twisted my hooked implement out and pulled it free.

The Fiend's face twitched, and beneath the stitched lids I could see the orbs of his eyes rolling in spasm. But I could hear the breeze whistling through the leaves above my head once more. Time was moving forward. The moment of danger was past.

I returned the head to the leather sack, stared into the leafy darkness and concentrated. One quick sniff told me that this was still a safe place. Nothing dangerous lurked in this copse that shrouded the summit of a hill and it was an excellent location. My enemies could not approach undetected.

My pursuers had gradually been increasing in

number, but I had lost them late in the evening, and soon after had employed some of my precious remaining magic to cloak myself. I had to use it sparingly because my resources were almost exhausted. Now it was nearly midnight and I intended to rest here and regain my strength by sleeping until dawn.

Some time later, I awoke suddenly, sensing danger. My pursuers were climbing the hill towards me and they had spread out to encircle the wood.

How could that have happened? I had cloaked myself well: they should not have been able to find me. I sprang to my feet and swung the leather sack onto my shoulders.

I had been running for too long. Now, finally, it was time to fight. The thought lifted my spirits; the anticipation of combat always did that. It was what I lived for: to test my strength against my enemies'; to fight and kill.

How many were there? I fingered the thumb-bones that hung from the necklace I wore around my neck, drawing forth their magical power before probing the darkness with my mind.

There were nine creatures approaching. I sniffed three times to gather more information. There were others further back – almost a mile away – maybe twenty or more moving in this direction. Something puzzled me and I sniffed again. There was a new addition to this larger group; someone or something with them that I couldn't identify. Something strange. What was it?

Something stronger and more deadly stalks you now.

That was what the Fiend had said. Was this what he was referring to?

Perhaps it was, but for now that whole larger group could be forgotten. First I had to deal with the more immediate threat, so I began to assess the level of danger posed by the group of nine.

Seven of them were witches. At least one of them was of the first rank and she used familiar magic. That might be how they'd found me. A witch's familiar could be anything from a toad to an eagle. Sometimes it was a powerful creature of the dark, although they were hard to control. So the familiar might have been able to find me despite the cloak I'd wrapped about myself.

I could also tell that one of the group climbing the hill was an abhuman – and that the ninth was a man; a dark mage.

It would be easy to make my escape by choosing the path of least resistance. Two of the witches were young – hardly more than novices. I could simply break through the encircling line at that point and flee into the darkness. But that was not my way. I had to remind them who I was. Send a clear message to all who pursued me that I was Grimalkin, the witch assassin of the Malkin clan. I had run for so long that they had grown disrespectful. I had to teach them fear again. So I called down the hill to my enemies.

'I am Grimalkin and I could kill you all!' I cried. 'But I will slay only three – the strongest three!'

There was no answer, but everything became very still and quiet. This was the calm. I was the storm.

* * *

Now I draw two weapons. In my left hand I grip the long blade that I use for hand-to-hand combat; in my right a throwing dagger. My enemies are entering the trees now, so I descend the hill, advancing to meet them. First I will slay the mage; next the abhuman; finally the familiar witch, the strongest of all.

I am walking slowly, taking care to make no noise. Some of my enemies either lack the skill to do likewise or are careless. My hearing is acute and I detect the occasional distant crack of a twig or the faint rustle of long skirts trailing through the undergrowth.

Once in position above the mage, I come to a halt. He is only a man and will be the easiest of the three to overcome. Even so, he is undoubtedly more powerful than six of the advancing witches. A witch assassin must never underestimate her opponent. I will kill him quickly, then move on to the next.

I coil myself like a sharp metal spring and concentrate on my attack, searching for the mage, probing the darkness with my keen eyes. He is a young man, but although his magic is strong, physically he is out of condition and overweight, breathing heavily from the climb.

I whirl into motion. Three rapid steps downhill, and I hurl the throwing blade without breaking my stride. It takes the mage in the heart and he falls backwards, dead even before he can cry out. His magical defences proved inadequate.

The abhuman is my next target. He is big, with wide-set eyes and sharp yellow fangs jutting up over his top lip. Such creatures – children of the Fiend and a witch – are immensely strong and need to be kept at a distance and tackled at arm's length. To fall into their grasp is to risk being torn limb from limb. They are invariably brutal and morally debased, the worst of them capable of anything. If my child had been such an evil creature I would have drowned it at birth.

I sprint towards him at full pelt, plucking another throwing knife from its leather sheath. My throw is accurate and would have taken him in the throat, but he has been protected. The witches have infused him with their power, creating wards that deflect my blade. It skitters away uselessly and he surges towards me, roaring in fury, wielding a large club in one hand and a barbed spear in the other. He swings the club and jabs with the spear. But I have moved before either reaches me.

The heavy sack bounces against my back as I change direction again. Then, with my long blade, I cut the abhuman's throat, and he falls choking, a stream of blood spraying upwards. Still without checking my stride, I run on.

Now I must deal with the third enemy – the familiar witch.

I am running widdershins, against the clock, so that my left and more deadly arm is facing towards the slope and the remaining witches, who are still moving upwards towards me. A witch attacks, but not the one I seek. I ram the hilt of my blade into her face and she falls back. She will live, but without her front teeth.

By now the powerful familiar witch has sensed my attack, and she turns to face me, sending dark enchantments like poisoned spears towards my heart. I flick them aside and head directly towards her. I hear the beating of wings and something swoops towards my face with claws outstretched. It is a small hawk – a kestrel. I sweep my blade upwards in an arc and the hawk screams, its feathers falling upon me like blood-flecked snow.

The witch shrieks as her familiar dies; she shrieks again when I cut her the first time. My next blow ends her life, and the only sounds now are the *slip-slap* of my feet on the ground and the *wish-swish* of my breath as I accelerate down the hill and leave the cover of the trees.

I speed eastwards out of the wood, leaving my enemies to find their dead. As I run, I go over in my mind what has happened. An assassin must evaluate both her successes and her failures; she must always learn from the past.

I consider again the means by which they have found me. The witch was powerful, but her familiar was just a small hawk. Their combined magic could not have seen beyond the cloak that I had cast about myself. No, it has to be something else.

What about the strange presence advancing with the larger group further back? What is it? Is it this that has discovered me? If so, it must be powerful. And it is something that I have never encountered before. Something new.

It is wise to be wary of the unknown. Its unfamiliarity makes it dangerous. But soon it will be dead. How can it hope to defeat me?

I am Grimalkin.

CHAPTER 2
AN UNKNOWN THREAT

Each day say to yourself that you are the best,
the strongest and the most deadly.
Eventually you will start to believe it.
Finally it will come true.
It came true for me.
I am Grimalkin.

Just before dawn I rested for an hour, drinking cool water from a stream and chewing my last few strips of dried meat.

My supplies were almost exhausted and I would need fresh meat to keep up my strength. Rabbits would have been easy to trap, but I was still being pursued and could not afford to rest for more than a few moments. The majority of my enemies were almost two miles back now, but one of their number had come on ahead of the group and was closing on me. It was the unknown creature that I had first sniffed back in the wood.

It was moving faster than I was. Whatever the danger it presented, soon I would have to turn and face it. But first I had to know more. So I took a small mirror from its sheath on my shoulder strap, muttered a spell, then breathed on it.

Within moments a face appeared. It was that of Agnes Sowerbutts. She was a Deane but bore no great love for her own clan. She lived apart from the life of Pendle and had helped me before. We had a bond between us – a common interest. She was the aunt of Alice Deane and a close friend of Tom Ward, the Spook's apprentice.

Agnes is skilled in the use of the mirror. Few are her equal in locating people, objects and dark entities. But she keeps herself to herself and few know that she is also a powerful scryer – far better than Martha Ribstalk, our greatest Malkin seer, who is now dead.

It was too dark for Agnes to read my lips, so I breathed on the mirror and made my request by writing on its surface. I wanted to know about the creature that pursued me.

**What pursues me?
What Will happen when I face it?
Can you help?**

I wiped the mirror. Agnes merely smiled and nodded. She would do her best to help.

So I ran on, trying to maintain the same distance between myself and my pursuer. The leather bag slapped against my back with each second stride. The Fiend's head seemed to be growing heavier by the hour. It was undoubtedly slowing me down. The pursuit was relentless, and gradually I was being overtaken. That fact did not displease me. Running like this was not my preferred option. I looked forward to the moment when I would have to turn and fight.

Dawn came, and with it grey skies and a chill drizzle drifting into my face. After about an hour I felt the mirror begin to move within its sheath. Agnes was trying to make contact, so I halted beneath the shelter of a large tree, lifted out the mirror and found Agnes's face staring back. It was a kindly face, with round cheeks and a plump chin, but one glance at her eyes told you that she was brave and not a woman to be trifled with.

Her name was Sowerbutts because she'd married a man from Whalley, leaving Roughlee, the Deane village, behind. Ten years later he died and she went home, but this time to live in a cottage on the outskirts of Roughlee. Although she liked to keep her distance from the clan, nevertheless she knew all their business. There wasn't much that went on in Pendle that escaped Agnes and her mirror.

She gave me a brief smile of welcome, but I could see the warning in her eyes before she spoke. It would not be good news. I concentrated, staring hard at her lips to read what was being silently mouthed at me.

What follows you is a 'kretch'. It was created by an alliance of witches, abhumans and mages specially to hunt you down and slay you. Its mother was a she-wolf, but its father was a daemon.

'Can you name the daemon?' I asked.

That knowledge was vital. I needed to know what powers it had. It would be wolf-like, but much would be determined by the gifts passed down from its father. My own clan, the Malkins, have also created kretches. The last one we named Tibb. We used it to try and counter the growing power of a seer from the Mouldheel clan. Kretches are usually created for a specific purpose. This one was supposed to kill me.

Agnes shook her head. *I am sorry*, she mouthed. *Strong magic cloaks that information. But I will keep trying.*

'Yes, I'll be grateful if you do that. But did you scry also? Did you see the outcome of my fight against this kretch?'

If you fight it soon, you will suffer a mortal wound. That much is certain, Agnes told me, her face grim.

'And if I delay that fight?'

The outcome is less clear. But your chances of survival increase as time passes.

I thanked her, replaced the mirror in its sheath and set off again at a sprint, trying to stay ahead of the kretch. As I ran, I thought over what Agnes had said. The fact that it was a kretch made me determined to elude it for as long as possible. Such creatures had short life-spans. It would age rapidly, so why face it in its prime? I had to keep the Fiend's head out of his servants' clutches. That was more important than my growing urge to turn and fight my enemy.

I did believe in the power of scrying, but it was not always accurate. In fact sometimes – though rarely – it could be inaccurate.

I remember my first consultation with Martha Ribstalk. Rather than using a mirror, her chosen method of scrying was to peer into a steaming blood-tainted cauldron in which she boiled up thumb- and finger-bones to strip away the dead flesh. At that time she was the foremost practitioner of that dark art.

As arranged, I visited her one hour after midnight. She had already drunk the blood of an enemy and performed the necessary rituals.

'Do you accept my money?' I demanded.

She looked at me disdainfully but nodded, so I tossed three coins into the cauldron.

'Be seated!' she commanded sternly, pointing to the cold stone flags before the large bubbling pot. The air was thick with the smell of blood, and each breath I took increased the metallic taste on the back of my tongue.

I obeyed, sitting cross-legged and gazing up at her through the steam. She had remained standing beyond the cauldron, so that her body would be higher than mine, a tactic frequently employed by those who wish to dominate others. But I was not cowed and met her gaze calmly.

'What did you see?' I asked steadily. 'What is my future?'

She did not speak for a long time. It pleased her to keep me waiting. I think Martha was annoyed because I had asked a question rather than waiting to be told the outcome of her scrying.

'You have chosen an enemy,' she said at last. 'The Fiend is the most powerful enemy any mortal could face. The outcome should be simple. Unless you allow it, the Fiend cannot come near you, but he will await your death, then seize your soul and subject it to everlasting torments. However, there is something else that I cannot see clearly. There is uncertainty – another force that may intervene; one which presents a faint glimmer of hope . . .'

She paused, stepped forward and peered into the steam. Once again there was a long pause. 'There is someone . . . a child just born . . .'

'Who is this child?' I demanded.

'I cannot see him clearly,' Martha Ribstalk admitted. 'Someone hides him from my sight. And as for you, even with his intervention, only one highly skilled with weapons could hope to survive – only one with the speed and ruthlessness of a witch assassin, only the greatest of all witch assassins – one even more deadly than Kernolde – could do that. Nothing less will do. So what hope have you?' Martha mocked.

At that time Kernolde was the witch assassin of the Malkins, a fearsome woman of great strength and speed who had slain twenty-seven pretenders to her position – three each year, as this was the tenth year of her reign.

I rose to my feet and smiled down at Martha. 'I will slay Kernolde and then take her place. I will become the witch assassin of the Malkins, the greatest of them all.'

Martha had laughed mockingly as I walked away, but I was perfectly serious. To defeat the Fiend I knew that I would have to develop my fighting skills and become the assassin of the Malkin clan. And then I would have to form an alliance with that unknown child.

Eventually I learned his name.

Tom Ward.

* * *

I hurried on, trying to pick up my pace. The drizzle had now become a torrential downpour, driving into my face and soaking me to the skin.

As I ran, I meditated on the art of scrying. Generally a witch uses a mirror, but some go into deep trances and glimpse the future through dreams. Some throw bones into the north wind and see how they land. It is also possible to cut open a dead animal and examine its entrails. But seeing into the future is uncertain, no matter what some scryers would have us believe. There is always the element of chance. Not everything can be foreseen – and a witch can never foretell her own death: another must scry it for her.

I disliked Martha Ribstalk, but she was good at her art and I consulted her many times after that first session. During our final meeting she predicted the time and manner of my death – she insisted that it would come about many years into the future, but I could not rely on that. Time has many paths: perhaps I have already taken one that made that prophecy void. If so, I know exactly what step that was.

I have allied myself with John Gregory and Thomas Ward. I have chosen to use my own dark powers to fight the dark and destroy the Fiend. That could change everything.

I was climbing now, my pace slowing. I reached a ridge and looked back in the direction of my pursuer. I crouched low so that the kretch would not see me against the skyline, and waited, eager to catch my first glimpse of it.

I did not have long to wait. I saw the beast created by my enemies emerge from a cluster of sycamores and leap a ditch before disappearing into a hedgerow. I saw it for only a second, but that was enough to tell me that I was dealing with something dangerous and formidable.

From a distance it looked, as I had suspected, like an enormous wolf. Just how big, it was difficult to estimate. It seemed to be loping along on four legs and was covered in black hair that was flecked with silver on its back. But then I realized that the front two limbs were really powerful, muscular arms. The creature was designed to fight and kill me. Everything about it would have been crafted to achieve one objective – my death.

It would be swift in combat, and very strong. Those arms would be like those of an abhuman, able to crunch my bones and tear off my limbs. No doubt its teeth and claws would be poisoned. One bite, or even a scratch, might be enough to bring about my slow, agonizing death. Perhaps that was what Agnes Sowerbutts had meant when she referred to the threat of a 'mortal wound'.

My instincts screamed at me to turn and fight now, to get it over with and slay this kretch. Pride bade me do the same. I wanted to test myself in combat against it. I would prove that I was stronger and better than anything they could send against me.

Oh, Mr Wolf! Are you ready to die?

But more was at stake here than my survival and my pride. In battle, chance often played a part. An ankle could be twisted by a stone hidden in the grass; an enemy less skilled than me might be favoured by a lucky strike. Malkin assassins had died like that before – bested by inferior opponents. I found it very difficult to imagine being defeated under any circumstances, but if I *did* lose, the Fiend's head would fall into the hands of my enemies, and before long he would walk the earth once more.

I had promised to keep the Fiend's head out of the clutches of his servants, so despite my lust for combat I would continue to run for just as long as I could.

CHAPTER 3
YOU ARE BLEEDING

Look – you are bleeding! Maybe close to death.
The pain is terrible.
Now your enemy approaches, ready to take your life.
Is this the end? Are you finally defeated?
No! You have only just begun to fight!
Believe me because I know.
I am Grimalkin.

As I ran on, I went through my options once more. In which direction should I go? So far my journey had been unplanned.

After following a long meandering path through Ireland, I had made a safe crossing from its eastern shores to the County by threatening a lone fisherman. After that voyage, most Pendle witches would have killed the man and taken his blood or thumb-bones. But I, the most dangerous of them all, had spared his life.

'You will never be closer to a violent death than you have been these past few hours,' I told him as I stepped onto the shore of the County. 'Go back to your family. Live a long and happy life.'

Why had I behaved thus? My enemies would see it as a weakness, evidence that I was growing soft and was ready to be taken – that I was no longer fit to be the witch assassin of the Malkin clan. How wrong they would be! He was no threat to me. When you kill as often as I am required to do, you grow weary of taking lives – especially the easy ones. Besides, the man begged. He had told me of his wife and young children and the daily struggle to keep them from starvation. Without him, he'd said, they would die. So I set him free and continued on my way.

Where should I go now? I could travel north into the

lair of the hostile water witches and weave my way through the hills and lakes, but those slimy hordes were loyal supporters of the Fiend. South was another option, but there a different danger awaited me. The forces that had invaded the County had only recently been driven south. It would be foolish to head towards their lines.

Yes, to keep moving was the best way to make sure that the head stayed out of the clutches of the Fiend's servants, but I needed to rest, and there was one place I could go that my enemies might not expect. I could return to Pendle, the home of my clan. Both friends and enemies awaited me there. Some witches were happy to see the Fiend loose in the world; others would like to destroy him or return him to the dark. Yes, I would head for Pendle – for a special place where I could take refuge while I rested, regained my strength and augmented my magical resources. Malkin Tower, once the stronghold of my clan, was now in the possession of two feral lamia witches – 'sisters' of Tom Ward's dead mother.

Would they allow me in? They were enemies of the Fiend, so perhaps I could persuade them to let me share that refuge.

It was worth a try, so I changed direction and ran directly towards Pendle.

However, long before I reached it, I realized that I would have to fight the kretch first. I had no choice. Better to turn and fight the enemy face to face than be brought down from behind. To continue running was no longer an option – the creature was now little more than a hundred yards to my rear and closing fast.

My heart began to beat faster at the thought of combat. This was what I lived for . . .

I paused at the top of a small rise and looked back. The kretch had just crossed the narrow valley below and was starting to lope up the hill, its black fur sleek with rain. Its eyes met mine and I saw more than eagerness there. It was frantic to sink its teeth into me, to tear my flesh and chew my bones. That was its sole purpose in life, and its desperate need for victory would add spice to our battle.

I placed the sack on the ground. I did not like to leave it unattended even for a moment, but I would fight more effectively if I was unencumbered. Now I must do everything right – everything to the best of my ability. My attack must be perfect. I would need magic as well as martial skills.

I reached for the necklace around my neck and began to touch each thumb-bone in turn, working from left to right. A monk fingers his beads one by one, using them as an aid to memory as he counts the circle of his prayers; my ritual is the muttering of each spell while drawing into my body the power that is stored within the bones. Each was a relic cut from the body of an enemy slain in combat. Each had been boiled with care until the flesh pecled off cleanly.

The initial spells – those of 'making' – have to be chanted accurately and with a precise cadence. If all is done correctly, the bones float to the surface of the cauldron and dance amongst the churning bubbles as if trying to leap out. Each is picked out by hand, despite the pain, and must not be allowed to fall to the ground. Then it is drilled through and added to the necklace.

The stronger the enemy, the greater the power that is now stored within each bone. But it is finite. Once a bone is drained of power, it must be replaced.

First I touched those of Janet Fox; she was strong and we had fought for two hours beneath the afternoon sun. I drew out the power that was left; now her bones would need to be replaced. The bones of Lydia Yellowtooth I didn't drain completely. She was subtle in combat – I needed some of that subtlety now, but chose to save a portion for later. So I continued to turn the necklace, fingering the bones. At last I had what I needed.

I was ready.

I run at full tilt towards the kretch. With every stride the rational part of me, my calculating mind, warns of just how difficult it will be to win here. The creature is far bigger than I estimated. Although in form it resembles a wolf, in size it is more like a small horse. In addition to those muscular arms with their long sharp-taloned fingers, there are pouches around its hairy body. These are not leather straps and sheaths; they are formed of its flesh, and weapons protrude from them.

But I have the instincts of a warrior and great self-belief. Whatever the odds, I will win. I am Grimalkin!

Without breaking stride, I stop my heart from beating. It is a skill that I have practised over the course of many years. My blood quietens: there are no peaks and troughs of surging circulation to spoil my aim. I draw a throwing knife from its scabbard and hurl the blade straight at the creature's head.

My throw is accurate and I find my target. However, to my annoyance and frustration, the blade does not penetrate the hide, but skids across the hairy head to fall harmlessly into the long grass. A metal helmet could not have provided a more effective defence.

Then I see a gleam of blood in the dark fur. I have

cut the flesh but the skull beneath is strong and thick, a bone barrier against my blades.

Surely the rest of the body cannot have similar defences? The movement of the sleek, lithe creature that runs towards me with such fluidity and grace says otherwise. There must be points of weakness. I will find them and the creature will die.

So I test its body, hurling a second blade straight at its flank. Its reactions are quick and it twists away so that the blade misses. I allow my heart to resume its beating.

Now the kretch rushes at me from a different angle. I am still sprinting forward and the long blade is in my left hand; this is the one I use for fighting at close quarters.

Matching me move for move, the kretch also draws a long blade from a pouch on its shoulder. It also uses its left hand. The talons of its right hand are ready to receive me too. But now I have decided exactly what to do. I know how I may swiftly win this battle and continue my flight with the Fiend's head.

There is a mighty clash as we come together; the kretch growls, showing its sharp fangs, and stabs towards my head. The stench of its rancid breath fills my nostrils as I duck under the blade and skid feet first beneath it. Sliding down the wet grassy slope beneath its furry body, I swing right and left with my blade, cutting into both hind legs, severing the hamstrings.

The creature gives a cry and collapses back onto its haunches, its blood spurting onto the grass. But I have already rolled clear, and I run back up the hill towards the leather sack, which I swing firmly up onto my shoulder. I look down the slope again and smile in triumph. The creature is howling, desperately trying to pull itself up the incline towards me with its strong forelimbs.

Oh, Mr Wolf! Now you are limping!

Its hind legs drag uselessly behind it. Thus hamstrung, it can never catch me now. No doubt its creators will find the beast and put it out of its misery. I am pleased with what I have achieved, but I had

41

expected the struggle to be more difficult. Yet it is good to triumph over my enemies.

My heart light now, I run on towards Pendle. I am filled with the exultation that comes from victory. Even the rain has stopped. There are gaps in the cloud and soon the sun will shine. As for my other pursuers, I have left them far behind.

I sat cross-legged on the grass and made myself comfortable. Next, I plucked the Fiend's head out of the sack and, holding it by the horns, placed it on a grassy bank so that it was almost level with my own. I removed the green apple and the thorns and waited patiently for our conversation to begin. It always began in exactly the same way.

'Unstitch my eyes!' the deep voice cried. The Fiend's words seemed to vibrate up through the grassy bank.

'Why repeat yourself? Will you never learn to accept your lot? Your eyes will remain stitched. Be grateful that I allow you a little time to speak. Don't waste it.

Have you anything to tell me? Anything worth listening to?'

The Fiend did not reply, but beneath the lids the eyeballs were moving frantically. Then the mouth opened as if he were speaking to someone, but I could hear nothing.

'Are you in communication with someone?' I demanded. 'Have you been conversing with one of your servants? If so, I will put you back in the sack!'

'My servants speak to me all the time, whether I am able to reply or not. They tell me things. I have just learned something very interesting.'

The mouth smirked as if relishing what it had been told, and dribbles of blood and saliva ran down its chin. I did not give the Fiend the satisfaction of asking what he knew. He was going to tell me anyway. I just had to be patient.

'It is done,' he said at last. 'You are finished – as good as dead. Soon I will be free.'

'I maimed the kretch that your servants created. So do not build up your hopes.'

'Soon enough you will see the truth, witch – very soon, in fact!'

'What? Truth from the Father of Lies?' said I, laughing contemptuously.

Always mindful of the Fiend's comfort, I plucked a big bunch of stinging nettles and spread them within the sack to make him a restful bed. Next, I thrust the green apple and rose thorns back into his mouth.

'Sleep well! Sweet dreams!' I cried, tying the string to bind him into the sack.

An hour before sunset I halted and set traps for rabbits. It was a warm pleasant evening and the grass had dried. I was already on the edge of Pendle District, and the hill itself was clearly visible to the northeast.

I decided to use my mirror to make contact with Alice Deane and see if she, Tom Ward and the Spook had reached the County safely. It was a week since I had last been in touch with her. At that time they had been about to leave the southwest of Ireland and travel overland by coach to Dublin to take a boat home. I was well ahead of them: I had already landed south of Liverpool and made my way northwards, keeping close to the coast before I'd had my first contact with the Fiend's servants west of Ormskirk.

Pulling the mirror from its sheath, I said the magical words of contact and waited patiently for Alice to appear.

The mirror brightened and she smiled out at me.

'I trust all is well?' I asked.

Alice nodded. *We've been home for three days, and Old Gregory has already got people working hard to rebuild his house. We're sleeping under the stars at the moment! How are you? Is the head still safe?* she mouthed.

'Yes, child,' I told her. 'There has been danger, but I have survived. The head is still safe in my hands – but I cannot run for ever. Tell Thomas Ward to put his thinking cap on! We need to destroy the Fiend – we must fix him permanently.'

I smiled at Alice and put the mirror away, staring towards the looming mass of Pendle.

I was almost home now. When I reached Malkin

Tower, would the lamias let me take refuge there? I wondered. If not, could I take it from them by force? Two together would be difficult to overcome, but if I entered by the tunnel I might be able to lure one down into the dungeons. In theory they were my allies, but if it proved necessary, I would kill them both.

I felt the mirror move again in its leather sheath. When I pulled it out, Agnes Sowerbutts was already staring at me. She looked concerned.

'I hamstrung the kretch,' I told her. 'That danger is past.'

I only wish that were so, Agnes mouthed back at me. *I spied the creature reflected in the surface of a small lake, where it paused to slake its thirst. Now it is following you once more with just the merest of limps. Soon it will be able to run freely again.*

I have now managed to scry the name of its father. The kretch was begat of Tanaki, one of the hidden daemons who are invoked rarely and only with great difficulty. Little is known of him, other than he has great perseverance. Once set on a course, he never deviates until his will is accom-

plished. Not only that: any defeat makes him stronger. Each time he fights he grows more formidable. Such traits will have been passed on to the kretch. It has been given great powers of healing.

I frowned and nodded. The hamstringing should have been permanent. This creature was going to be very difficult to overcome. I could no longer allow myself the respite of a night's sleep.

There is worse, Agnes said, looking directly at me, her lips moving silently. *Your forehead is cut . . .*

I reached a finger up to my brow and, to my dismay, traced the line of a gash. My finger came away faintly smeared with red. It was little more than a scratch, no doubt inflicted by one of the kretch's talons. In the heat of the fight I hadn't felt a thing. I remembered that Agnes had scryed that I would suffer 'a mortal wound'.

'Surely this small scratch is nothing?' I said.

The wound is slight. But poison may have entered your bloodstream. Would you like me to scry again and see the outcome?

47

I felt quite well and hardly thought it was necessary, but to please Agnes I nodded, and the image in the mirror faded. I spent the next hour cooking and eating two plump rabbits while I thought about the kretch. Just how cleverly had my enemies crafted the creature? Maybe the glands at the base of its claws secreted a substance that stopped its victims feeling pain? This was a trick employed by some predators so that their prey failed to seek attention for the poisoned wound . . . until it was too late. But I was still not overly concerned. Filled with new energy, I ran on through the night towards Pendle. I felt strong. I had no symptoms of poisoning at all.

Not then.

They began just as the brooding shape of Pendle loomed up out of the murky pre-dawn light.

It started with a disturbance to my vision. Tiny flashes of light appeared at the corners of my eyes. I had never experienced anything like it before and at first I paid little heed. But gradually the flashes grew worse: I then became breathless and my heart-rate increased. I tried to ignore these symptoms – along with the sack, which seemed to be growing heavier with every stride. Then my legs started to feel unsteady.

Suddenly I was on my knees as a wave of nausea shook me. I vomited my supper onto the grass and crouched there, retching and gasping for air. After a few minutes my breathing returned to something approaching normal and I struggled to my feet. But when I tried to run, my legs felt like lead and I could only stagger forward a few steps at a time.

Within minutes my condition began to deteriorate further. Each ragged breath that I sucked desperately into my lungs brought a sharp pain. But I couldn't afford to stop. I imagined the kretch picking up its pace and loping after me. Even if my progress was slow, every painful step would take me nearer to Pendle. Physically I was exceptionally strong and resilient. My self-belief remained strong: I was sure that I could fight off the effects of the poison.

The mirror moved: I took it out and gazed upon the

face of Agnes Sowerbutts once more. Her expression was grim and she shook her head slowly.

The poison is slow-acting but deadly, she mouthed. *Without help, you will probably soon be dead. But I cannot tell what will befall you: as I scryed, the mirror went dark.*

There was still room for hope, I thought – a darkening mirror merely meant that things were uncertain.

'Could you help me?' I asked.

I'm an old woman and can't travel to meet you. But if you come here I'll do my very best to help.

Agnes was a powerful healer. If I could only reach her cottage . . .

I thanked her, then returned the mirror to its sheath. My whole body was shaking now. I tried to deny it but could not escape the truth. I knew I didn't have the strength to reach the outskirts of the Deane village alone.

I had always been self-sufficient; mostly I had walked alone. Pride now reared its head up before me, a barrier between me and the help that I needed. Who could I ask anyway? Who could I trust? Above all I needed someone to carry the Fiend's head and keep it out of the hands of the kretch.

I had no true 'friends' amongst the clans, but there were those I had helped or formed temporary alliances with – witches such as Alice Deane. Unfortunately Alice was too far away to help. She was back at Chipenden with John Gregory and Tom Ward.

I went through the list of the ones I might be able to trust, but quickly dismissed them in turn. Pendle's clans had been split into three groups when they had summoned the Fiend to walk the earth: there were those who served him, those who opposed him and, finally, those who watched and waited, perhaps planning to ally themselves with the winners of the conflict.

I had been away from Pendle for many months and there was no way I could be sure of anyone now. I stared towards the grey mass of Pendle Hill, my mind circling like a moth around a candle flame, going anywhere but into that inevitable fire.

There was one person I could ask for help, but she

was young and I didn't want to endanger her. However, she was also strong and was well able to assist.

Witch assassins are not like spooks; traditionally they do not take apprentices. But I am not like previous assassins. I trained a girl in secret. Her name?

Thorne.

CHAPTER 4
KILL THAT BEAR!

That beast has arms strong enough to tear you limb
from limb, a fanged mouth big enough to bite off your head.
What chance have you against such a foe?
None at all; you are as good as dead.
I know the answer; it is simple:
kill it from a distance!

Thorne sought me out five years ago when she
was just ten years old. I was sitting cross-legged
under an oak tree close to Bareleigh village and
meditating on my next task: to seek out and kill
something that wasn't human. In the forest northeast
of Pendle a bear had turned rogue and had killed three

humans in the last month. There were few bears left in the County but it had to die.

I was not aware of the approach of danger because I did not recognize it in one so young.

The child came very close to me and kicked me hard on the thigh with the toe of her pointy shoe. In a second I was on my feet. I lifted her by her hair and dangled her so that her face was close to mine.

'If you ever do that again,' I warned her, 'I will slice off your foot!'

'I'm brave,' she said. 'Don't you agree? Who else would dare to kick the witch assassin?'

I looked at her more closely. She was just a slip of a thing with hardly any meat on her bones, but she had a determination in her eyes that was very unusual in one so young. It was as if something much older and more powerful glared out of that young face. But I wasn't going to take any nonsense from her.

'You're more stupid than brave!' I retorted. 'Be off with you. Go back to your mother – there'll be chores for you to do.'

'Don't have a mother or a father. I live with my ugly uncle. He beats me every day.'

'Do you kick him?'

'Yes – and then he beats me even harder.'

I looked at the girl again, noting the bruises on her arms and the dark mark under her left eye. 'What do you want of me, child?'

'I would like you to kill my uncle for me.'

I laughed and set her down on the ground, then knelt so that we were eye to eye once more. 'If I killed your uncle, who would then feed and clothe you?'

'I will work. I will feed myself. I will become a witch assassin like you.'

'To become the witch assassin of our clan you will need to kill me. Are you capable of that? You're just a child.'

Traditionally, each year three witches were trained to challenge the incumbent clan assassin. But no one had confronted me for many years. After slaying the fifteenth pretender, I had put a stop to the practice, having grown sick and weary of slaying challengers. It was a foolish waste of lives that was gradually bleeding away the strength of the Malkin clan.

'Soon I'll be as big as you but I won't kill you,' the girl said. 'You will die one day, and then I'll be ready to replace you. The clan will need a strong assassin. Train me!'

'Go home, child. Go back and kick your ugly uncle even harder. I will not train you.'

'Then I will come back and kick you again tomorrow!'

With that, she left, and I thought no more about it, but she returned the next day and came to stand before me. I was in my forge, sharpening a new blade.

'Did you kick your ugly uncle again?' I asked, unable to prevent a smile creeping across my face as I rested the completed blade on the anvil.

The child did not reply. She stepped forward and tried to kick me again, but I was ready. I slapped her hard and threw her down into the dirt. I wasn't angry, but I'd had enough of her foolishness and wanted to show her that I was not to be trifled with. But the girl was stubborn and – yes – she was brave. She attempted another kick. This time I snatched up my blade and pointed it at her throat.

'Before the end of the day, child, this new blade will taste blood! Take care that it isn't yours!'

Then I threw her over my shoulder and carried her off towards the forest. It was late afternoon when I found the tracks of the bear; dusk when I reached its lair, a cave in a wooded hillside. There were bones outside, scattered across the loam. Some of them were human.

I could hear the animal scuffling about inside its den. It soon caught our scent and moments later emerged on all fours. It was big, brown and fierce; blood was smeared across its snout and paws. It had been eating but still looked hungry. It glared at us for a moment, and I stared back hard and hissed at it to provoke it. It reared up on its hind legs and gave a terrible bellow of anger.

I set the girl down on the ground at my side. 'What's your name?' I demanded.

'Thorne Malkin.'

I handed her the blade I'd forged and sharpened that morning. 'Well, Thorne, go and kill that bear for me!' I commanded.

She stared at the bear, which was now lumbering towards us, its mouth open, ready to charge. For the first time I saw fear in her eyes.

'It's too big,' she said.

'Nothing is too big to be killed by a witch assassin. Slay that bear for me and I will train you. Then one day you will take my place.'

'What if it kills me?'

I smiled. The bear was now getting very close. 'In that case I will wait until the bear starts to eat you. Once it is distracted I will kill it.'

Something happened then that was completely unexpected. By now the child was shaking with fear and looked ready to flee at any second. This was exactly what I wanted. My intention was to cure her of the folly of wishing to become a witch assassin.

And she *did* run, but not in the direction I expected.

Thorne lifted the blade, gave a yell and ran straight towards the bear.

When I drew and hurled another blade, she was just seconds away from death. I rarely miss and my aim was perfect, the dagger burying itself up to the hilt in the bear's left eye. It staggered and started to fall – but Thorne was still sprinting towards it. As she stabbed it in the left hind leg, the dead animal collapsed on top of her.

She was lucky not to have been killed, or at least seriously hurt by such a weight falling on her. When I dragged her out, she was covered in bear blood but otherwise unhurt. I had been impressed by the courage displayed by one so young; she deserved to walk away unscathed.

'I killed it!' she exclaimed triumphantly. 'Now you have to train me.'

I lifted the head of the bear and pointed at the dagger embedded in its left eye.

'*I* killed it,' I told her. 'You merely offered it supper. But now we'll have a supper of our own. This bear has dined on human flesh for quite a while; now we will eat its heart.'

I was as good as my word. While Thorne collected wood, I took what I needed from the bear: its heart and two tender slices from its rump. Soon I had a fire going and was cooking the meat on a spit. Once it was done I cut the heart in two and handed half to the girl.

'It's good,' she said. 'I've never tasted bear meat before.'

'There are very few bears left, but just in case you ever confront another, there are a couple of things you ought to know. Never stab it in the leg – it only makes it angry. And never get in close. Such an animal must be killed from a distance. They are immensely strong: once a bear has hold of you, you're as good as dead. They can tear off your limbs or crush your skull with one bite.'

Thorne chewed her meat thoughtfully. 'I'll remember that the next time we go bear-hunting,' she said.

I almost laughed out loud at the presumption of that 'we', and I smiled at her. 'You were afraid, child, and yet you obeyed me and attacked the bear. So yes, I will begin to train you. I will give you a month to prove yourself.'

I picked up the new blade that Thorne had used to stab the bear. 'Here,' I said, handing it to her, 'this is yours now. You have earned it. This is your first blade.'

Thus I began to train Thorne, but I did so in secret. There were three reasons for that. Firstly, if any of my enemies knew of it, the girl would become a target. By capturing or hurting Thorne they might seek to bring pressure to bear upon me.

Secondly, I was jealous of my reputation and wished to continue to inspire fear for my ruthlessness and independence. It was for this reason that I carved the image of scissors on trees.

Thirdly, the successor to the Malkin witch assassin had traditionally been chosen through combat. I judged it best that after my death the practice should continue once more: witches would then compete with each other for the title; I did not wish it to look as if I was personally selecting my protégée as my successor.

If Thorne became the next assassin, she would have to earn the position in the conventional manner. I had no doubt that she would do so.

The month passed quickly and all was to my satisfaction. The girl was courageous, and obedient too – the latter was important. I prefer to work alone, but with a partner I must be in charge and there is no room for wayward behaviour.

I remember the first time Thorne showed her true worth and I realized just how good an assassin she might one day become.

Water witches dwell in the far north of the County. They are no friend to the Pendle covens and they had recently killed a Malkin witch who had been travelling south through their territory. I had been despatched by my clan to kill three of their number in retaliation.

Thorne took no part in the slaying of the water witches. She was there to watch and learn. I killed three, as directed; then, choosing a clearing in the forest, I placed their heads on stakes, carving the sign of my scissors on the surrounding trees. Thus there could be no mistake. It was not just for vengeance; it was a warning.

With hindsight I realize that I should have left immediately afterwards and sped back to Pendle. Instead Thorne and I spent a useful day on the shores of the lake some call Coniston It was a day of training and I pushed the girl hard. The sun had just gone down behind the trees when we began her knife training. I was trying to teach her to be calm and control her anger. She had the blades; I used my hands.

'Cut me!' I shouted, slapping her face and stepping back out of range.

Thorne whirled towards me, wielding two blades, slashing at me, her face full of fury. I stepped inside her guard and slapped her even harder; twice this time, stinging both cheeks and bringing tears to her eyes.

'Keep calm, girl! It's only pain!' I mocked. 'Think! Concentrate! Cut me!'

She missed again, and I gave her another hard slap. We were close to the water's edge and by now it was twilight; tendrils of mist snaked towards us over the lake's surface.

Thorne took a deep breath and I saw her face relax. This time she feinted, and the arc of her first blade came so close that I felt its breath whisper over the skin of my shoulder. I smiled in appreciation and took a rapid step backwards to avoid her next thrust. I was inches from the water's edge and the lake was deep.

The attack came suddenly, taking us both by surprise. I had my back to the water and Thorne saw the creature first. Her eyes widened in shock, and I turned and glanced back over my shoulder, seeing the death that was surging towards me.

The beast had arms and long fingers with sharp talons, but it was more fish than man, with a nightmare face and cold cod eyes, a mouthful of sharp teeth and a long, sinuous, eel-like body with a narrow fin.

I tried to twist away, but it surged up out of the water, riding on its tail, seized me by the shoulder and yanked me backwards. As my head went under the cold water, I realized that I had no blade at my disposal. I had been fighting Thorne unarmed and my leather straps, sheaths and knives were spread out on the grass some distance from the water's edge.

But I wasn't finished yet, and with the nails of my left hand I gouged out the creature's right eye; then I bit through its fingers to the bone. However, it was immensely strong and was dragging me deeper and deeper into the murky water. I hadn't had time to snatch a deep breath and realized that I was now in serious trouble.

But then I saw another shape in the water beside me and felt a knife being pressed into my hand. I used it quickly – to good effect. And I wasn't alone. Thorne was by my side, and together we cut that creature to pieces.

At dawn we assembled its remaining fragments beside the lake. I had never seen anything quite like it before, but it was without doubt an abhuman. They take many strange forms, and this one had been adapted for an aquatic life. The Fiend sometimes uses such creatures to destroy his enemies. He cannot come near me, so he'd sent one of his children instead.

Without doubt Thorne saved my life that day; it had required great courage to join me in the water like that. As a reward I boiled up the creature's thumb-bones and gave them to her. They were the first bones that she hung on her necklace.

Back in Pendle, I customarily trained Thorne several times a week and occasionally took her with me when I set off on long journeys, seeking out those marked for death by my clan.

I had watched her develop from a young eager girl into a potential witch assassin who would one day take my place. Because of the war and my journey to Ireland, it was several months since I had last seen her, but I knew she would be ready to answer my call.

I stared into the mirror now and chanted the incantation. Within moments Thorne's face came into focus. Gone was the child who had charged at the bear. She had gentle eyes, each iris a vivid sapphire blue, but her lean face was that of a warrior, with a wide mouth and sharp nose. Her dark hair was cropped short and she had a small tattoo on her left cheek: the effigy of a bear. She'd had it done to remind her of the day I had agreed to train her.

You're hurt! she mouthed, showing her teeth. *What happened?*

I had forbidden her to file her teeth to points until her training was fully completed, so her rare smiles were not yet terrifying to others.

I told her about the kretch and the poison, but it was the severed head of the Fiend that concerned me most, and I explained what I had in the leather sack. That was the real reason why I was reluctantly summoning Thorne into such great danger.

'Whatever happens, it must not be allowed to fall into the hands of the Fiend's servants,' I continued. 'If I die, you must take over that burden.'

Of course, but you're not going to die. Where are you?

'Southwest of Pendle, about five miles from the base of the hill.'

Then hold on – I'll be with you very soon. How far behind you is the kretch?

'It's impossible to be sure,' I told her, 'but probably only a few hours at the most.'

Then try to keep moving. Remember what you once said to me – 'You have only just begun to fight.'

With that, the mirror darkened and Thorne was gone. Fighting against the pain, I struggled to my feet and began to stagger eastwards once more, my breathing hoarse and ragged. My progress was very slow and I began to imagine that I could hear the kretch padding through the trees behind me, getting closer and closer, ready to spring.

At one point I whirled round to meet it, but there was nothing there. The next thing I remember is lying on my back with rain falling straight into my face. I opened my eyes in a panic.

Where was the leather sack? I reached out for it but found nothing.

'It's safe – I have it beside me,' said a voice I knew.

Thorne was kneeling beside me looking concerned. I tried to sit up but she gently pushed me back down again.

'Rest,' she said firmly. 'Give the potion time to take effect. I called in to see Agnes on my way here. What she sent is not a cure but it should buy you some time. After you spat out the first mouthful I managed to pour most of it down your throat.'

'The kretch – is it close?' I asked.

Thorne shook her head. 'I can't sniff its approach.'

'If we can reach Pendle we'll be safe for a while. The witches who made the creature are from the southwest of the County. They will not dare venture into our territory.'

'I hope you're right,' said Thorne. 'But the clans are divided. Some may allow them entry. Now, try to stand.'

69

She helped me to my feet, but I was unsteady and she had to support me. Although only fifteen and not yet fully grown, she was now almost as tall as me and looked every inch a witch assassin. She was dressed in a similar fashion to me – leather straps crisscrossed her body, the sheaths holding blades.

I smiled at her. 'I'm still not strong enough to travel. Leave me and take the sack. That's what is really important.'

'We'll travel together,' Thorne said firmly. 'Remember how you once carried me?'

'When we hunted the bear? Yes, I remember it well. I was thinking about that earlier.'

'Well, now I'll carry you.'

With that, Thorne hoisted me up onto her shoulder and, carrying the leather sack in her left hand, began to jog eastwards. We were heading towards Agnes Sowerbutts's cottage on the outskirts of the Deane village of Roughlee.

It was strange to be carried in this way. I was at war with myself: one part of me felt anger at my weakness and resentment towards Thorne for treating me thus; the other felt gratitude for her help and was well aware that the skill of Agnes Sowerbutts would give me the best possible chance of surviving.

After a while the stabbing pain in my lungs started to return as the effects of the potion began to wear off. The agony slowly intensified until I could hardly breathe and I felt myself losing consciousness again.

The next thing I remember is what sounded like the eerie cry of a corpse-fowl very close by. Then there was a sudden stillness and a change of temperature. I was no longer being carried; I was inside, out of the rain. I lay on a bed and someone was bending over me; the concerned face of Agnes Sowerbutts swam into view.

I felt my head being lifted, and suddenly my mouth was full of a vile-tasting liquid. I swallowed a little and almost vomited. I wanted to spit the rest out but fought to control my urge. Agnes was trying to help me. She was my only hope of survival. So I forced myself to swallow again and again. After a while a strange warmth spread slowly from my stomach to my extremities. I felt comfortable. I think I slept for a while.

But then I was awake again, my body racked with pain. There were sharp twinges in my chest, and each breath was like a dagger stabbing into my heart. My limbs throbbed and felt as heavy as lead. Whatever potion Agnes had given me, it hadn't worked for long. I opened my eyes but could see nothing. Everything was dark. Had the poison taken away my sight?

Then I heard Agnes's voice: 'The poison is too virulent. She's dying. I'm sorry but there's nothing more that I can do.'

CHAPTER 5
MALKIN TOWER

Blood, bone and familiar magic work for most witches,
but the old ways are not the only path to power.
There is nothing wrong with tradition,
but I am open-minded and flexible.
I am Grimalkin.

'Please, please, try again,' I heard Thorne beg. 'She's still fighting, still strong. Grimalkin deserves another chance.'

I fought to stay awake, but eventually I lost consciousness again, falling slowly into a darker, deeper sleep than I had ever known before.

Was this death? If so, Thorne was alone. How long

would she be able to keep the Fiend's head out of the hands of his supporters? I had told her a little of my alliance with Alice Dean, Tom Ward and John Gregory. Would she understand that she needed to approach them directly and seek their help?

I tried to call out to Thorne and tell her what must be done, but I was unable to speak. I was trapped deep within my body, forced to endure the pain, which was increasing all the time.

I wasn't going to remain lying here in agony while my body slowly lost its grip on life. There was a way to escape the pain. I could float out of my body to meet my death. I had some skill in the arts of shamanistic magic.

Most Pendle witches are deeply conservative in their habits: at an early age they are tested by their clan to determine which type of dark magic – blood or bone or familiar – they have an aptitude for. They would never think to range beyond those options. But I am different. My mind is flexible and open to other alternatives. I am willing and eager to learn new things.

This may be because during my life as a witch assassin I have travelled widely and have encountered other cultures and ways of utilizing the dark. One such encounter was with a Romanian witch who was living in the northeast of the County. It was she who taught me something of shamanism.

Of course, you could spend a lifetime learning its secrets and practising its craft. I had but a few months to devote to it, so I concentrated on just one aspect of its repertoire – the skill of projecting the soul from the body.

Such a procedure is not without risks. One practitioner, a mage, projected his soul into the dark and was devoured by a daemon. You may also be unable to find your way back to your body. For that reason I had used it only rarely, and with great caution.

But what did it matter now? I was dying. The mists of Limbo would close about me soon enough, whether I left my body or not. At least I would be able to see again – after a fashion.

The process usually involves a few key words

muttered in a particular cadence, but equally important is the *will* to escape.

I had lost control of my body and couldn't even move my lips to speak the words of the spell. As it was, my will, driven by desperation, proved sufficient. Moments later I was floating just a few feet above the bed upon which my body lay. Thorne was sitting in a chair, her head in her hands. The leather sack was within her reach. A candle flickered on the small table beside her.

I looked down at my weary face, mouth open to suck in rapid shallow breaths. I had never thought it would end this way. It didn't seem right. Grimalkin was never meant to die in a warm bed – she should have met her end in battle, as a warrior. But on reflection I realized that I had. The kretch had killed me. That scratch from its poisoned talon had been the moment of my defeat – the beginning of my death.

I floated away and passed through the closed door. I was nothing more than a small glowing orb of light, invisible to most people. The strongest of witches and spooks might be able to glimpse me, but only in a very dark place. Even candlelight made me almost totally invisible.

However, I could see clearly, even in the dark – though only one colour was visible. Everything was a shade of green, and living things glowed, lit by the life-force within them. The front room of Agnes's cottage was exactly as I remembered it: cosy, clean but cluttered. The walls were lined with shelves full of books or rows of jars containing ointments, dried herbs and withered roots. First and foremost Agnes was a healer.

She was sitting on a stool by the fire in the small front room, reading a book. I drifted closer and read the title on the spine: *Antidotes to Deadly Poisons*.

So she had listened to Thorne and hadn't given up on me yet. Even though my enemies had created a kretch specially designed to kill me, it did not necessarily mean that they had concocted a totally *new* poison. The creature itself would have used up much of their strength and resources, at great cost to themselves. It had been endowed with many means with which to kill me, and poison was just one; they might simply have selected one of the most deadly. If Agnes could determine which one it was, I might still have a chance.

I floated on, passing through the wall of the cottage with ease. Ahead lay the huge long mass of Pendle Hill. I sped on swiftly. I might die at any moment but I had to keep my hopes up. There was something that I could do now that, were I to recover, might help me to keep the Fiend's head safe.

I had decided to visit Malkin Tower and see what the situation was there – where exactly the two lamias resided. I flew towards Crow Wood and was soon swooping low over the treetops, invisible to the fierce carrion crows that roosted below on their leafy branches.

A bright green half-moon cast its sickly light upon the tower. It was a grim fortification, surrounded by a moat, topped by battlements and protected by a huge iron-studded door. It had once been the home of the

Malkin coven, but now the two feral lamias dwelt there. Before the war and the enemy occupation, I had been instructed by the coven to kill them and retake the tower. I had refused, telling them that the lamias were too strong and that the attempt would lead to my certain death.

One of the coven had twisted her face into a sneer. 'I never thought the day would come when Grimalkin would consider an enemy too strong!' she'd jibed.

In retaliation, I broke her arm and glared at each of the other witches in turn. They were afraid of me, and they quickly cast down their eyes.

But I had lied. Fully armed and fit, I felt confident that I could defeat the lamias – especially if I could engineer a fight with them one at a time and in a place of my choosing. However, for now it suited my purposes to have them inhabiting the tower. For within lay the chests owned by my ally, Thomas Ward, one of which contained knowledge and artefacts belonging to his mother: these might one day aid us in our struggle against the Fiend and his servants. With the lamias as guardians, the chest and its contents were safe.

Had I been approaching clothed in flesh, I would have used the tunnel that led to the dungeons far below the tower, and climbed up into it that way. Meeting a hostile lamia in a confined space would have been to my advantage. The two guardian lamias could fly, and it would not be wise to meet them in the open.

Shortly after the coven had completed the ritual to raise the Fiend, I had taken part in the battle fought atop Pendle Hill. We were attacked by a rabble from Downham village and would have made short work of them – but the intervention of the lamias was decisive. Despite the accuracy of my blades, they persisted in their attack. My knives found their targets half a dozen times, but the lamias' scales were a better defence than the toughest armour. Many witches had died that night.

As I approached the moat, I felt a tug as if I were being pulled back towards my body. Never had I travelled so far from it. The thin invisible cord that bound me to it could snap and bring about my death immediately. That had always been my fear. Maybe this was why some shamans failed to find their way back and died: they had gone too far and snapped the cord . . . But did it matter now? I was close to death anyway. Unless Agnes found a cure, little time remained to me.

I crossed the moat and passed through the thick stone of the tower to find the living quarters in a state of disarray, just as they had been when the soldiers had used their eighteen-pounder gun to breach the walls.

My clan had escaped through the tunnels, leaving their meals half eaten. Since then, during a brief occupation by the Mouldheels, the breach had been fixed – before the lamias had driven them out in turn. The floor was strewn with rubbish, and in the adjacent storeroom lay sacks of rotting potatoes and mouldy carrots, so it was fortunate that my spirit was unable to smell. Spiders' webs covered in clusters of desiccated flies were strung from every corner. Cockroaches and beetles scuttled across the flags.

And there amongst the rubbish was the large locked chest that had belonged to Tom's mother. It was safe.

All at once I noticed something that made me wonder. The chest was free of cobwebs. It wasn't even dusty. And beside it stood a small pile of books. Had they been taken from the chest? If so, who had been reading them?

Because it had been guarded by the lamias, Tom Ward had left the chest unlocked. But someone had been here very recently, and no doubt they had delved inside. I felt a surge of anger. Where were the two lamias? How had this been allowed to happen?

I floated up the stairs and out onto the battlements, where I saw two more trunks; they had once contained the dormant bodies of the lamias. Abandoned, both were open to the elements and were covered in moss, like the stone flags beneath them. With everything appearing in shades of green, it was hard to tell whether the wood of the boxes was rotten or not.

I gazed out over the surrounding countryside. On every side the tower was surrounded by the trees of Crow Wood. All was still and silent. But suddenly I heard a distant cry that sounded like the shriek of a corpse-fowl, but somewhat deeper – as if it came from the throat of a much larger creature. Then a dark shape flew across the face of the green half-moon. It was a lamia heading back towards the tower.

She swooped towards me – four feathered wings, black-scaled lower body, talons gripping something. She circled the tower twice, then dropped her prey onto the battlements close to where I was hovering. It hit the flags with a dull thump, and blood splattered across the flags. It was a dead sheep. The lamia had been out hunting. But where was her sister? I wondered.

The creature swooped towards the tower again, and instinctively I reached for my blades. Then I remembered my present state. Even clothed in flesh this would not have been a good place to face the lamia.

She landed on a trunk, curved talons gripping the

wood – which was clearly not rotten. The creature was formidable, and would be difficult to defeat even if she could not fly. She was bigger than I was – maybe nine or ten feet tall if she ever stood upright. Those rear limbs were strong and taloned, able to carry a heavy weight such as a sheep or cow, but the forelimbs were more human, with delicate hands that could grip a weapon; the claws were slightly longer than a woman's fingernails but exceedingly sharp – able to tear open a face or slice into a neck.

The lamia gazed directly at me and I suddenly realized that she could see me. It was night, but the moon was surely casting enough light to make me invisible. Either she had exceptionally keen sight or she was using powerful dark magic.

The creature opened her mouth to reveal sharp fangs, and spoke to me in a hoarse, rasping voice:

'Who are you, witch? What do you want here?'

I was unable to reply. Perhaps there was a way for a disembodied sprit to communicate, but it was a shamanistic skill that I had never learned. And I was puzzled by the fact that this feral lamia could actually speak. It suggested that she was beginning to shape-shift slowly back to her 'domestic', almost human form; in this shape, only a line of green and yellow scales running down the length of her spine betrayed her true nature.

'Sister, I think we have a spy here. Send her on her way!'

The feral lamia was no longer looking at me; she inclined her head, with its heavy-lidded eyes, towards the doorway.

I turned to follow her gaze. A woman was standing there, staring straight at me. I looked more carefully and realized that in fact she was more beast than woman. The other lamia had already shape-shifted to a point where she had arms and legs and stood upright. However, she was still a monstrous thing and had some way to go to complete the transformation. She breathed heavily, like a predatory beast about to spring, and her arms were too long – the hands hung well below her knees. The face was savage, but there was intelligence in the eyes, and the high cheekbones showed the beginnings of beauty.

She cried one word, '*Avaunt!*' – hurling it against me with palpable force.

It was a word from the Old Tongue; a spell. The alternative words for that dark spell are '*Be gone*'. She was driving me away and, in my spirit form, I had no power to resist.

I felt a tightening of the invisible cord that bound me to my dying body, and I was snatched backwards from the battlements. But not before I had seen something else.

The other lamia was holding a leather-bound book in her left hand. Was it something that she had taken from Tom's mother's trunk?

Suddenly I was being dragged back over the trees of Crow Wood. Everything became a blur, and with a thud I was back in my body and felt pain again. I tried to open my eyes but I was too weary. Then I heard another thud and realized it was the beating of my heart. It was a slow, ponderous beat; it seemed to me that it was about to fail, weary of keeping the blood coursing through my dying body.

My life as a witch assassin was over. But I had trained Thorne well. There was someone to take my place.

I closed my eyes and fell into a deep darkness, accepting death. It was over and there was nothing more that I could do.

CHAPTER
6
THE LAMIA GIBBET

Malkin Tower is the dark spiritual home of our clan.
Many grieve its loss but I care nought,
for each place I fight is home.
My blades have a home too –
in the hearts of my enemies.

But that was not the moment appointed for my death. I awoke to find Agnes bathing my forehead.

She smiled and helped me up into a sitting position, placing pillows behind my back.

'I've been in a really deep sleep,' I said.

'Yes – a coma that lasted almost three days.'

'I'm cured?' I asked. I felt weak and a little

light-headed, but the fever had gone and I was breathing normally. My brain was sharp and clear – I felt alert.

The smile died on her face. 'I'm not sure that "cured" is the right word,' she said. 'After much trial and error I finally found an antidote and it saved you from death. But whether you will make a *full* recovery is uncertain.'

'What do you mean by that?' I demanded. Then I became aware of the anger and hostility in my voice. 'Forgive me,' I said. 'Thank you for saving my life.'

Agnes nodded. 'I did my very best,' she continued, 'but sometimes, even though a poison is cleared from the system, damage remains. There may be permanent weakness. The lungs, heart or other internal organs may be affected. Sometimes the damage is permanent; there may be periods of illness, while at other times the victim's health is nearly normal.'

I took a deep breath, trying to take in what Agnes was telling me. The implications were obvious. My role as a witch assassin depended on my strength and physical fitness. Without that as a certainty I would be vulnerable to attacks that would not previously have bothered me.

'So you think that I am permanently damaged?'

Agnes sighed. I could see that she was choosing her words very carefully. 'I think that is likely. I have never seen anyone suffer such extreme poisoning as yours and make a full recovery.'

I nodded. 'Thank you for being candid. I can only hope that I will be the first to do so. I will certainly try to become again what I was formerly. Now tell me – where is Thorne? I trust that the head is still safely in her possession?'

'It is safe. She's in her room now, sleeping with her left hand gripping the sack, as always. But there are threats beyond these four walls. It won't be safe to stay here much longer. The witches who control the kretch demanded entry into Pendle but were refused. However, some here offered their support, and there have already been skirmishes between the rival groups. A big battle is imminent; if those opposed to the Fiend lose, the kretch will come here to hunt you down.'

I nodded. 'Then it's better if I leave as soon as possible.'

'Where will you go?'

'I will go to Malkin Tower, where even the kretch will not be able to reach me. Once inside that fortification, the Fiend's head will be beyond the reach of our enemies.'

'What about those who guard it?'

'We'll deal with them if necessary.'

'You'll take Thorne with you?'

'Yes. She's just a girl and I don't like to lead her into such danger, but what choice do I have? The contents of that sack are more important than anything else. Besides, the lamias may allow me entry. After all, I am their ally.'

'They may take some convincing of that. Feral lamias are a law unto themselves and don't always think logically.'

'The situation has changed. One of them is now closer to the human than the feral state. The other one, although still able to fly, can speak. They are both now shape-shifting towards the domestic form.'

'How do you know that?' Agnes asked. 'I have seen a lamia circling the tower but couldn't probe its defences. They have erected strong magical barriers.'

I didn't answer. A witch keeps such things to herself and never tells others more than is necessary. No doubt Agnes too had secrets of her own.

I swung my legs over the edge of the bed and Agnes helped me to my feet. I felt shaky but was able to walk unaided into the front room. I sat down on a stool close to the fire while Agnes prepared some broth. After a few minutes Thorne came out of her bedroom carrying the leather sack. Her mouth opened in surprise, and then she smiled and sat on the floor at my feet.

'It's really good to see you up and about,' she said.

'Hardly that, child. At the moment all I have strength for is to sit on this stool. But yes, death will have to take me another day.'

'You'll feel stronger once you get this inside you,' Agnes said, handing me a bowl of broth. 'But I think you'll need to spend at least another day here before you're fit to travel anywhere.'

I nodded. She was right. Desperate as I was to reach the sanctuary of Malkin Tower, it would be foolish to attempt it in my present condition.

The following night, after thanking Agnes again, we took our leave and I led the way towards Malkin Tower. We walked slowly because I still felt weak, but my breath came easily enough now and I was free from pain.

Soon the village of Roughlee was far behind us and we could see Crow Wood in the distance. But that wasn't where we were heading – at least not directly.

Our first destination was the entrance to the tunnel that led into the tower's dungeons. Once known only to the clan leader, its location was now common knowledge in Pendle, but the presence of the lamias kept even the most powerful witches at a distance. We entered the thicket of trees that enclosed what had once been a graveyard. Tombstones leaned at crazy angles and there were treacherous holes in the ground, hidden by undergrowth – empty graves from which the bodies had been removed before the ground had been deconsecrated.

There, ahead of us, bathed in pale moonlight, stood the ruin of a sepulchre, its roof split asunder by a young sycamore tree which shadowed its roof and single door. I pulled a small black wax candle from my thigh pocket and muttered a spell that flared it into life. Thorne did likewise, and I led the way into the burial chamber, pushing my way through the curtain of spiders' webs. Scattered on the floor lay human bones that had been dislodged from their resting place by those who had gained access to the tunnel; above them, six stone shelves housed the remains of the dead – all members of a once wealthy local family. Now they shared the luxury and riches of death.

I crawled across the lowest shelf into the space between this and the slab above, and made my way into the tunnel. There was a musty smell of damp earth and the roof was very low, forcing me to crawl on all fours. I glanced back, and Thorne gave me a grin. She had long wanted to explore these tunnels and enter the tower. Now she would get her wish. I only hoped that the cost would not be too high. For long minutes we moved slowly forward. It was difficult because I had to push the heavy leather sack ahead of me as well as keeping the candle alight, but at last we emerged into an earthen chamber. Directly opposite was the opening of another tunnel, but this was much larger, with roof supports.

'Shall I take the lead for a while and carry the sack?' Thorne asked.

'By all means take the lead, child, but the sack is my burden.'

She came forward, sniffed the entrance for danger and, with a quick nod, went in.

I followed without hesitation. I trusted her judgement and at present she was probably fitter, stronger and more alert to danger than I was.

95

After a while we came to a pool of stagnant water, its surface the colour of mud. Here there had once dwelt a dark creature called a wight, created by the Malkin coven to guard the tunnel. A wight is the large bloated body of a drowned sailor; it is animated by its soul, which is bound to the will of its creators. Such a creature is usually blind, its eyes having been eaten by fishes before the body was salvaged. It hides under the water and, upon sensing the approach of an interloper, reaches up to grasp the ankle of its victim, which it drags beneath the surface and drowns.

Wights are strong and dangerous, but this one had been slain by one of the lamias, who had ripped its body to pieces. Now all that remained was a faint stink of rot and death. We picked our way along the narrow slippery path that bordered the water and moved on further into the tunnel. As yet there was no hint of danger, although the lamias could well be lurking somewhere ahead, out of normal sniffing range. I could have used my necklace bones to probe further, but I needed to conserve my finite store of magic.

We reached a stout wooden door set in the stone, hanging wide open upon its hinges. This was the entrance to the dungeons. In the days when this was a Malkin fortification, it would have been securely locked.

After sniffing for danger, Thorne led the way inside and we stepped into a dark, dank passageway flanked on either side by cells. Water dripped from above and our footsteps echoed on the damp flags. All the doors were open and no living prisoners remained, but by the flicker of our candles we saw that some contained human bones, with partial skeletons dressed in mildewed rags still manacled to walls. Many had limbs missing, bitten off and dragged away by the hordes of rats that used to frequent the dungeons. There was no sign of them now, and I soon found out why.

We reached a large, high-ceilinged, circular chamber, with stone steps curving upwards to a jagged hole. There had once been a trapdoor that gave access to the floor above, but the lamias had enlarged the opening to afford them easy access. My gaze quickly moved from that to the circle of five stone supporting pillars. Each was hung with manacles and chains – this was where prisoners had been tortured. The furthest pillar – the one next to a wooden table covered in instruments such as knives and pincers – was different.

At its foot was a large wooden bucket into which blood was dripping. Thirteen chains hung down from the darkness above: each terminated at a different height; each bore a dead creature. There were rats, rabbits, hares, a fat badger, a kestrel and a black and white cat. Most were dead, their life blood having long since drained into the bucket. But two, both large grey rats with long whiskers, still twitched as their blood slowly leaked out, drop by drop.

'Why would a lamia do this?' Thorne whispered, her eyes wide.

'This is a lamia gibbet . . . its true purpose is unknown. Some think they are a warning to others, but there may well be another significance. No doubt enough blood eventually accumulates in the bucket to make it worthwhile,' I answered, 'but lamias can hunt and kill much larger prey – sheep, for example. Maybe they enjoy the taste of such small creatures. Some Pendle witches actually prefer a rat's blood to a human's. But if this is so, why the thirteen chains? That suggests a ritual. Perhaps it's some type of lamia magic,' I speculated.

As we stared at the grisly spectacle, we both suddenly sensed danger and glanced up towards the hole in the ceiling. I sniffed quickly. 'The lamia – it's the winged one!' I warned.

A second later, something large dropped down towards us. It fell fast, wings held close to its body, like a hawk swooping towards its prey.

CHAPTER 7
PROMISE ME

Why kill the weak when you can fight the strong?
Why tell a lie when you can speak the truth?
A witch assassin should be honourable,
and always keep a promise.

At the last moment the lamia spread her wings wide, soared away from the wall and began to circle the chamber. Then she swooped towards us again.

Thorne drew a blade. I shook my head. 'Don't be a fool!' I cried, grabbing her arm and dragging her in the direction of the narrow passageway. We would be better off there than in this huge chamber, where the lamia could attack us from above. I remembered how my blades had bounced of her scales in the battle on Pendle Hill.

We reached the entrance of the passage and stepped inside. The lamia landed in the very centre of the chamber and started to scuttle towards us on all four limbs. This type of winged lamia, known as *vaengir*, was relatively rare but extremely dangerous. It would be better to negotiate than fight – but I would kill her if necessary.

She halted less than six feet away and stood up on her muscled hind limbs, stretching her forelimbs towards us threateningly. I knew that such creatures could move very quickly. She could be upon us in a second. So I put down the sack, stepped in front of Thorne and drew my long blade.

But rather than attacking us, the lamia spoke. 'Who are you, witch? You are foolhardy to enter our domain for a second time!'

Thorne looked at me in astonishment. I had not told her that I had visited the tower in spirit.

'I am Grimalkin, the assassin of my clan, the former owners of this tower. I come in peace. I am an ally of Thomas Ward and therefore yours too. We oppose the Fiend – he is our mutual enemy.'

'And who is the child who cowers to your rear?'

Thorne stepped forward and pointed her blade towards the lamia. 'I am named Thorne and I serve Grimalkin. Her will is my will. Her enemies are my enemies. Her allies are my allies. I cower before nothing and fear nothing!'

'You speak bravely, child. But courage alone will not protect you from my claws and teeth.'

'You would not threaten us if you truly knew who Grimalkin is,' Thorne snapped. 'She is the greatest Malkin assassin who has ever lived. None of her clan now dare challenge her. Some enemies have died of fear in their beds after hearing that she hunts them down.'

'I already know of her fearsome reputation,' said the lamia, 'but I have lived for centuries and the telling of my deeds would exhaust the breath of a thousand minstrels. What brings you both to this tower?'

'We seek refuge for a while,' I answered. 'Our enemies pursue us. But we fear nothing for ourselves; our terror is that this should fall into their hands.'

I held up the sack. 'This contains the severed head of the Fiend. I have impaled his body and buried it in a pit far from here across the sea. Our enemies wish to reunite the two parts and restore his strength. Tom Ward seeks a way to finally destroy him, but we need to gain time for him to do so. The head must remain safe.'

The eyes of the lamia closed for a moment as if she were deep in thought. Then she nodded slowly and pointed a taloned forefinger up towards the hole in the ceiling. 'We sensed the binding of the Fiend and his pain. All who serve the dark felt that the very moment it was accomplished. I would see this head, and so would my sister. Follow me up into the tower.'

With those words she leaped into the air and soared

aloft. Moments later she had flown out of sight through the hole.

'It might be a trick,' Thorne said. 'Once we're in the open she could well attack.'

I nodded. 'But it's a chance we'll have to take,' I said and, picking up the sack and holding the candle aloft, I passed between the nearest two pillars and began to climb the spiral staircase.

Scrambling up through the jagged hole in the ceiling, we emerged into the huge underground cylindrical base of the tower. Of the lamia there was no sign. Water dripped from above, no doubt seeping into the stones from the moat. Cautiously, we continued up the narrow spiral steps, which were slippery and treacherous. On our left was the stairwell, and to fall would result in certain death; on our right was the curve of the wall, and set into it at intervals were doors, each a dank dark cell to hold prisoners. I peered into them all but they were empty even of bones.

At last we reached what had once been the upper of the two trapdoors; this too had become a jagged hole in the stone to make passage for the lamias easier. We emerged into the storeroom, with its sacks of rotting potatoes and a stinking, slimy mound of what had once been turnips. When I had visited this place in my spirit form I had been spared the stench, but it was now overpowering; even worse than when the tower was occupied by the Malkin coven. Torchlight flickered beyond the doorway, which led to the large living area.

Holding our candles up, we walked through. The winged lamia was perched on the closed trunk, and on a stool nearby sat her sister, holding a book in her left hand. A torch set in the nearest wall-bracket lit the left sides of the two witches, casting their shadows almost as far as the wall. Most of the huge room lay in darkness.

'Here are our two guests, sister,' the winged lamia rasped. 'The young one is called Thorne. The taller one, with death in her eyes and cruelty in her mouth, is Grimalkin, the witch assassin.'

The witch on the stool attempted to smile at us but

only managed to twist her face into a grimace. Her teeth were slightly too big to fit into her mouth and she breathed noisily.

However, when she spoke, her voice was soft, with no hint of harshness. 'My name is Slake,' she said. 'My sister is named Wynde, after our mother. I believe you have something to show us?'

I placed the leather sack on the floor and untied it. Then I slowly drew forth the Fiend's head and held it up by the horns so that it was facing towards the lamias. They both smiled grotesquely at the sight.

'The green apple is a clever way to ensure silence,' said Slake approvingly.

'I like the way it is wrapped in thorns,' added Wynde.

'But why don't you simply destroy the head?' Slake asked. 'We could boil it up in a cauldron and eat it.'

'Better to eat it raw,' Wynde rasped, fluttering her wings, her bestial face suddenly showing excitement. 'I'll have the tongue, sister. You can have the eyes!'

'I have already considered destroying it but I dare

not!' I interrupted. 'Who can know the consequences of such an act? This is not simply a witch to be returned to the dark for ever by the simple expedient of eating her flesh. We are dealing with the dark personified, the Devil himself. To eat the head might liberate him. He can change shape, make himself small or large at will. Once free, he has terrible powers – some perhaps still unknown. I have pierced his body with silver spears; thus is he bound and his power taken away. It is safer to keep the head intact yet separate, so that his servants cannot remove the spears and reanimate him.'

'You are right,' Slake said. 'It would be foolish to take a chance when so much is at stake. We loved our dead sister dearly and have promised to protect her son, the Thomas Ward of whom you spoke. But tell me – is he any nearer finding a sure way to destroy the Fiend?'

I shook my head. 'He is still searching and thinking. He wondered if there was something in that chest that might help.'

Slake smiled, showing her teeth, and tapped the book she was holding. 'I have been sorting through the chest with that same object in mind – to finish the Fiend for ever. So far I have found nothing. Perhaps while you stay with us you would care to help?'

I smiled and nodded. The lamias had just offered us refuge. 'I will be happy to help,' I said. 'But no doubt we'll soon have enemies at our walls.'

'Let them come and enter my killing ground below the walls of this tower,' Wynde said. 'It will be good sport – the best hunting for many a year!'

Thorne and I ate well that night. Wynde, the winged lamia, snatched another sheep and dropped it onto the battlements for us; she had already drained its blood. I butchered it there and brought the most succulent pieces inside to cook on a spit.

The ventilation in the chamber was poor and smoke went everywhere. Not that it bothered me: my stinging eyes brought to mind the many happy hours I'd spent here as a child, watching the coven's servants prepare and cook their meals.

'Who was the very first person you killed?' Thorne asked as we tucked into our late supper.

I smiled. 'You already know that, child. I have told you this story before – many times.'

'Then tell me again, please. I never tire of it.'

How could I deny her? Without Thorne's help I would be lying dead to the west of Pendle. So I began my tale.

'I wanted to hurt the Fiend badly after what he had done to my child, and I knew where and when I'd be most likely to find him. At that time the Deanes were his favourite clan, so at Halloween I shunned the Malkin celebration and set off for Roughlee, the Deane village.

'Arriving at dusk, I settled myself down in a small wood overlooking the site of their sabbath fire. They were excited and distracted by their preparations, and I'd cloaked myself in my strongest magic so had little fear of being detected. Combining their magic, the

Deane witches ignited the bone and wood fire with a loud *whoosh*. Then the coven of the thirteen strongest formed a tight circle around its perimeter while their less powerful sisters encircled them.

'Just as the dead-bone stink of the fire reached me, the Deanes began to curse their enemies, calling down maimings, death and destruction upon those they named. Remember, child, that curses are not as effective as a blade. Someone old and enfeebled might fall victim to them, but mostly they're a waste of time because all competent witches have defences against such dark magic.

'Soon there was a change in the fire: the yellow and ochre flames turned brilliant red – the first sign that the Fiend was about to appear. I heard an expectant gasp go up from the gathering and I brought all my concentration to bear, staring into the fire as he began to materialize.

'Though he was able to make himself large or small, the Fiend now appeared in his fearsome majesty in order to impress his followers. He stood in the fire, the flames reaching up to his knees; he was tall and broad – perhaps three times the size of an average man – with a long sinuous tail and the curved horns of a ram. His body was covered in thick black hair, and I saw the coven witches reach forward across the flames, eager to touch and stroke their dark lord.'

'How did you feel?' Thorne asked excitedly. 'Were you nervous, or even a little afraid? I certainly would have been! You say now that you fear nothing, but you were young then – no more than seventeen – and you were about to attack the Fiend within sight of an enemy clan.'

'I was certainly nervous, child, but also excited and angry. If there was fear within me, it was buried so deeply under those other emotions that I was unaware of it. I knew that the Devil would not stay in the flames for long. I had to strike now! So I left my hiding place among the trees and began to sprint towards the fire. I came out of darkness, a blade in each hand, the third gripped tightly between my teeth. I hated the Fiend and was ready to die, either blasted by his power or torn to pieces by the Deanes.

'So I cast my will before me. Although I had the power to keep him away, I did the opposite now: I willed him to stay. I ran between those on the fringe of the gathering. As the throng became denser, I pushed the witches aside with my elbows and shoulders, surprised and angry faces twisting towards me. At last I reached the coven and threw my first dagger. It struck the Fiend in the chest and buried itself up to the hilt. He shrieked long and loud. I'd done some damage, and his cry of pain was music to my ears. But he twisted away through the flames so that my next two blades did not quite find their intended targets; but, even so, they pierced his flesh deeply.

'For a moment he looked directly at me, his pupils vertical red slits. I'd nothing with which to defend myself against the power that he could summon. Worse, he would be certain to find me after my death and inflict never-ending torments on my soul. So I willed him away. Would he go? I wondered. Or would he destroy me first? But he simply vanished, taking the flames of the fire with him so that we were plunged into absolute darkness. The rule had held. I had carried his child so he could not remain in my presence; not unless I wished it.

'There was confusion all around – shrieks of anger and fear; witches running in all directions. I slipped away into the darkness and made my escape. Of course I knew that they would send assassins after me. It meant I'd have to kill or be killed.

'I hurried north, passing beyond Pendle Hill, then curved away west towards the distant sea, still running hard. I knew exactly where I was going, having planned my escape far in advance: I would make my stand on the flatlands east of the River Wyrc's estuary. I had wrapped myself in a cloak of dark magic but knew that it was not strong enough to hide me from all those who followed me. Some witches have a special ability that allows them to see through such a cloak. So I needed to fight in a place that would give me the advantage.

'There is a line of three villages there, aligned

roughly north to south and joined by a narrow track that sometimes becomes impassable because of the tide. On all sides they are surrounded by bog and soggy moss. The river is tidal, with extensive salt marshes, and northwest of Staumin, right on the sea margin, stands Arm Hill, a small mound of firm ground which rises above the grassy tussocks and treacherous channels along which the tide races to trap the unwary.

'On one side is the river, on the other, the salt marsh, and nobody can cross it without being seen from that vantage point. Any witch who ventures there suffers great pain, but I gritted my teeth and made the crossing and waited for my pursuers, knowing there would be more than one.

'My crime against the Deane clan was terrible. If they caught me, I would die slowly and in agony.

'The first of my enemies came into sight at dusk, picking her way slowly across the marsh grass. As a witch, I have many skills and talents. One of these proved very useful now. It is a gift that we share,

Thorne. As an enemy approaches, we instantly know their worth; their strength and ability in combat. The witch crossing the marsh towards me then was competent, but not of the first order. No doubt her abilities as a tracker, which also enabled her to penetrate my dark magical cloak, had brought this one to me first.

'I waited until she was close, then showed myself to her. I was standing on that small hill, clearly outlined against the fading red of the western sky. She ran towards me, clasping blades in each hand. She did not weave from side to side; made no attempt to present a difficult target. It was me or her. One of us would die. So I pulled my favourite throwing knife from my belt and hurled it at her. My aim was good. It took her in the throat. She made a small gurgling noise, dropped to her knees and fell face down in the marsh grass.

'Yes, child, she was the first human being I had ever killed, and there was a momentary pang in my chest. But it quickly passed as I concentrated on ensuring my own survival. I hid her body under a shelf of grass tussocks, pushing her down into the mud. I did not take her heart. We had faced each other in combat and she had lost honourably. One night that witch would return from the dead, crawling across the marsh in search of prey. As she posed no further threat to me, I would not deny her that.'

'If I die before you,' Thorne said, 'promise me that you *will* take *my* heart. I prefer to go directly into the dark. I don't want to linger on as a dead witch, shuffling around the dell, waiting for pieces of my body to fall off.'

I nodded. 'If that is your wish I will not deny you. But if I die first, leave my heart intact. Hunting from the dell is better than suffering eternal torment in the dark at the hands of the Fiend. If we do not destroy him, one day he will be waiting for me – and for you too now, Thorne. Are you sure you don't want to reconsider?'

Thorne shook her head. 'We will find a way to destroy him, and then we can go safely into the dark, where we belong. One day I will be reborn into a new body: I will become a witch assassin once more and try to surpass all that I have achieved in this life!'

I smiled. Witches returned not only as dead vampiric creatures; they could sometimes also be reincarnated into a brand-new body and live a second or even third life.

'Now complete your story, please,' urged Thorne. 'They sent others after you, didn't they?'

I nodded. 'Yes, I waited almost three days for the next to find me. There were two, and they arrived together. We fought as the sun went down. I remember how it coloured the river red; it looked as if it was filled with blood rather than water. I was young, strong and fast, but they were veterans of such fights and knew tricks that I had never even imagined, never mind encountered. They hurt me badly, and the scars of those wounds mark my body to this day, but I learned much during that fight. The struggle lasted over an hour and it was very close, but at last victory was mine and the bodies of two more Deanes went into the marsh.

'It was almost three weeks before I was fit to travel, but in that time they sent no more avengers after me. The trail had gone cold and it was unlikely that anyone would have recognized me that night when I stabbed the Fiend.'

'Even to this day, the Deanes don't know that it was you, do they?' Thorne asked.

'That's true, child – you are the only one I've told this tale to. Let's hope they never find out or my days as a witch assassin would be over. I would be hunted down by a whole clan. They would never forget.'

CHAPTER 8
WHAT AILS YOU, AGNES?

A witch assassin of necessity walks alone.
The allies she makes are few in number;
thus they are valued highly,
their loss keenly felt.

Soon Thorne fell asleep by the fire. Of the lamia sisters there was no sign. They had gone into the underground region of the tower – for what purpose I could not guess. So I climbed the steps up onto the battlements. No moon was visible, and the wind was rising; heavy clouds blew across the sky from the west. So I penetrated the darkness, gazing out across the clearing towards the encircling trees of Crow Wood with my witchy eyes.

I could see the roosting crows and spied a badger rooting around close to his sett, but apart from that nothing moved. I sniffed three times to be sure, but there was no danger.

That was strange. I would have expected to find at least one enemy spy out there.

Satisfied, I crossed the battlements again and began to descend the steps. Suddenly lights began to flicker in the corners of my eyes. I felt dizzy, and the sack containing the Fiend's head seemed to grow much heavier. The world spun around me. I almost fell headfirst but managed to drop to my knees. Everything grew dark and my heart thudded ponderously. I took slow, steady, deep breaths until my vision cleared at last.

As the moment of weakness passed, I came slowly to my feet. Was this the long-term damage that Agnes Sowerbutts had warned might be a result of my poisoning by the kretch? If I suffered such a spasm during a fight with an enemy, I would certainly be killed. It was terrible to be compromised in this way. I had always had a great belief in my skills and my ability to overcome any opponent and dominate each situation. Suddenly my world had changed. I was no longer totally in control.

Shaken, I sat down at the foot of the steps and rested for a while with my head on my knees. I must have fallen asleep because the next thing I remember is sensing the movement of my mirror in its sheath. It was in my hand before I'd opened my eyes.

Agnes's face came into focus. For a moment I thought she had scryed what I had experienced and was contacting me to offer advice. But then I saw the expression of fear on her face and knew that something was very wrong. She mouthed words at me so quickly that I had to concentrate hard in order to read her lips:

A fierce battle has been fought just south of Roughlee and the supporters of the Fiend have won. They have invited the kretch and its creators to join them in Pendle and they will soon combine to destroy you. Even Malkin Tower may not be safe. Flee north while you can!

'But what ails *you*, Agnes?' I asked softly. 'I can see your lips trembling with fear.'

They are coming for me, Grimalkin. For what purpose I cannot scry. When I try, despite all my skill the mirror grows dark. It is well known that a witch is unable to foresee her own death. I was consumed with grief when my poor husband died and I will never be as happy as I was when living with him. But I have grown used to my situation – at least I am warm and comfortable. I hoped to have many more years ahead of me. I am not ready to die yet.

'Listen, Agnes, leave your cottage immediately and head towards the tower. It doesn't matter how slow your progress. I will find you and carry you safely within.'

It's too late! Too late for me! I hear them banging at my door now. Outside there are many witches. I can hear their yells of anger! I am about to die!

All at once the mirror went dark. Agnes was in the hands of our enemies and now there was nothing I could do to help. But I would avenge Agnes and repay my enemies thrice over for everything they did to her.

At dawn, up on the battlements, I told the others about Agnes and what I had learned. It was starting to rain, and now I could sniff out enemy witches lurking amongst the trees.

'Why did they go directly to Agnes's cottage to seize her?' Thorne asked.

'Despite the fact that she kept herself to herself, no doubt it was already common knowledge amongst the Deanes that she was not a supporter of the Fiend. But there were others they could have taken first – some more active in their cause. I suspect that they used a scryer to link her to me. Perhaps they know that we visited her cottage and that she helped me. If this is so, they will know about you too.'

Thorne shrugged. 'It was only a matter of time before they found out anyway. You could not keep me a secret for ever – certainly not from witches. But surely we can do something?' she insisted. 'We owe

Agnes a lot. Over the last four years she's been like a grandmother to me – and a true friend. We must help her. I cannot bear the thought of her being alone and afraid, in the cruel hands of merciless enemies! How can we stand by and allow this to happen?'

I shook my head. 'There will be too many of them. And she may already be dead. I am sorry about Agnes – she was indeed a good friend to me too – but to keep the Fiend's head out of their clutches is our main concern.'

'But Agnes is our concern too! We owe her much. I can't believe that you are prepared to allow her to die! You are Grimalkin! Don't forget that. Or has the kretch's poison made you less than you were?'

'Be silent!' I commanded. 'Yes, we owe her, but we have another greater priority. Obey me in this or I will train you no longer!'

'Soon the time will come when you'll have nought left to teach me!'

I smiled mockingly, showing her my teeth. Sometimes Thorne wound herself up so tightly that she exploded with rage. It was in her nature, but she had to learn discipline and be reminded of her place.

In that moment she attacked.

She sprang to her feet and directed a kick at my left shoulder. I caught her foot and twisted, and she came down hard. But she was up again and on me in an instant. We rolled together on the wet flags, Thorne fighting like a wild cat, scratching and biting.

I let the battle continue for a few moments so that she could release her anger and tension, then I put an end to the nonsense. I thrust a finger hard into each of her nostrils and dragged her up onto her feet. Still keeping my grip, I slammed her hard against the outer wall of the tower next to the steps, driving the breath from her body. I twisted her head away from me, opened my mouth wide and prepared to bite her throat. I would not hurt her badly, but a little pain would teach her a lesson.

At the last possible moment she drummed her left foot three times against the wall. It was the sign of submission, so I released her. She stood there swaying, her face pale. Blood mixed with mucus dribbled from her left nostril. But as usual after such a struggle, her eyes were shining. We stared at each other until, after a few seconds, the corners of her mouth twitched up into a smile.

I nodded to her and went to sit down again. The two lamias were looking at us in astonishment. But it was nothing new. We had fought together many times; it was part of Thorne's training. From time to time I need to demonstrate to her what her true position was. As well as being reckless, the girl sometimes got above herself.

'I will go and see what is afoot,' Wynde declared. Then she launched herself from the battlements and swooped towards the trees. She circled the tower three times, then gained height before flying south towards Roughlee.

We waited in silence with water dripping from our hair. When Wynde returned ten minutes later, the news was not good. She landed gracefully, then scuttled down the steps out of the rain and perched on the chest, waiting for us to climb down to her.

'What did you see, sister?' Slake demanded.

'Many witches heading towards Crow Wood, all carrying weapons – but they come to their deaths,' Wynde declared, water running off her wings to form a big puddle on the flags. 'I have had some sport already.'

I glanced down and saw that her hind feet were freshly stained with blood and that there were streaks of it in the water below the chest. She had already killed at least one of our enemies. I felt frustrated that I was unable to kill some of them myself. It was a great advantage to have wings.

'Do you think they mean to attack? Maybe they'll come up through the tunnel?' Thorne suggested.

'They'd have to reach the entrance first,' Wynde said.

'A few might be able to get inside. The thicket around the sepulchre would offer cover,' I said. 'But we could easily defend the tunnel. Just one of us could hold them off. We are in no immediate danger.'

'Then I will go down there now,' said Slake. 'I will stay until dusk, when another should take my place.'

I nodded in agreement and the lamia crossed into the storeroom and went down the steps to the lower reaches of the tower.

'If only Agnes had managed to get here,' said Thorne. 'I wonder what's befallen her. I can't stop thinking about what they are doing to her.'

Just before noon we found out. We were watching from the battlements when a score of witches strolled out of the trees and headed directly towards us. Wynde prepared to take to the air and attack but I bade her wait a while.

'Why must I wait?' she demanded, fixing me with her savage eyes.

'Because they have Agnes with them as a prisoner and she still lives,' I said, pointing to a figure to the fore of the group approaching the tower. I glanced sideways at Thorne, watching her eyes widen with concern at my words. I knew that whatever happened next would be bad, and we would be forced to bear witness to it.

Agnes was bound, her hands tied behind her back and a noose around her neck; the rope was in the hands of a black-bearded mage who walked ahead of her. I would have expected to see terror on Agnes's face but she seemed calm. Was she aware of the imminence of her own death, and had she therefore become resigned to it? Or did she hope to be rescued – perhaps by the winged lamia?

My attention was then drawn back to the mage. I sniffed quickly three times. Instantly I knew a lot about him. He was capable of powerful dark magic and was also the leader of those who had created the kretch. Additionally, he was a skilled warrior, his strength such that in combat I would have to be wary of him. Only a fool would underestimate such a mage.

'I will kill that one next!' Wynde said.

'If I had your wings I'd do it now!' hissed Thorne.

'Hush!' I commanded them both. 'Let us listen to what he has to say for himself.'

They came right up to the edge of the moat and halted. Immediately the mage looked up at us and called out his demands in a loud, imperious voice.

'I am Bowker,' he shouted up at us, 'the appointed leader of the Fiend's servants. You have until sunset to give us what is ours. If you refuse, the first to die will be your friend and ally, this old witch. She likes peering into mirrors too much! Her death will not be easy.'

He turned and led the group back towards the trees, tugging roughly on the noose around poor Agnes's neck – her groan of pain was clearly audible. Wynde fluttered her wings, preparing to take flight and attack.

'No!' I warned. 'If you attack, he will slay Agnes immediately.'

The lamia shook her head. 'He will kill her anyway. Once back amongst the trees the advantage will be theirs. I must strike now while they are still in the open!'

She took off from the battlements, gained height, then swooped down towards the group of witches, attacking them from the rear. There was a scream of pain as Wynde soared aloft again. She was carrying one of the enemy witches, whom she released when she'd risen to twice the height of the surrounding trees. Whether or not her victim was already dead was impossible to say, but there was no scream as she fell, and the body thudded heavily onto the ground.

The lamia's attack was reckless. By now the mage might already have cut Agnes's throat. Of course, such feral creatures are a law unto themselves and she certainly did not share my regard for Agnes, who had just recently saved my life.

The lamia killed twice more before the group reached the cover of the trees. Losing the advantage of flight, Wynde headed back towards us and landed on the battlements.

'Why didn't you attack the mage?' I demanded. 'With him dead you might have been able to carry Agnes to safety.'

The lamia regarded me with her heavy-lidded eyes. There was blood on her lips and cruelty in her gaze. 'The mage had a weapon – something I've never encountered before. He held a small rodent's skull in his fist, and when he pointed it at me, my balance went awry and I almost plummeted to earth. I could not get near him without the risk of falling out of the sky.'

I nodded but said nothing. The damage was done. What it would cost Agnes Sowerbutts was impossible to say. I expected them to kill her anyway.

At dusk the screams began.

CHAPTER
9
IS SHE A COWARD TOO?

A witch should not fear her own death.
It is just the setting of a sun
and a promise of the darkness
which is our true home.

They were torturing Agnes and there was nothing I could do to help. Thorne covered her ears and started to moan.

'Poor Agnes!' she exclaimed. 'What has she done to deserve this?'

'Nothing, child. But you don't have to listen. Go down to the tunnels and relieve Slake of her guard duty. I will change places with you soon after dawn.'

I spent the remainder of the night watching from the battlements with the two lamia sisters, Wynde scratching her talons against the flags in frustration. Just after dawn the screaming stopped. Then they threw a body out from under the trees. It landed on the edge of the clearing. Even from this distance I could see that it was Agnes.

'I'll go and collect her,' Wynde said.

'Take care – it could be a trap!' I warned her, simultaneously wishing that I could do something – anything rather than remain as a spectator. I itched to fight and avenge Agnes's death. But it was very likely that our enemies would be waiting just within the trees. If the mage used his skull weapon, causing Wynde to fall, dozens of them could surround her within seconds.

But with her usual impetuousness, the lamia flew down from the battlements and snatched up the body. She soared back towards us and laid it gently at my feet.

Agnes was dead, her eyes wide open and staring.

Her clothes were in tatters and the torturers had left their marks on her poor aged body.

'They haven't taken her heart,' Wynde said. 'I could carry her to the dell. Is that what she would want?'

I didn't know what Agnes wanted because we had never spoken of it. Hunting from Witch Dell as a dead witch was attractive to some. Others, such as Thorne, found it abhorrent and preferred to go directly to the dark. I wasn't sure, but a decision had to be made so I opted for the dell. I hoped I'd done the right thing.

'Yes, please carry her body there and bury it close to the centre. Make a shallow grave and cover it with leaves.'

With strong flaps of her wings, Wynde climbed above the tower in a slow spiral, then flew north towards Witch Dell, a dark speck against the grey sky, slowly diminishing into the distance. Within the hour she returned and told me that she had buried Agnes beside a large oak tree right at the heart of the dell.

I thanked her, then went down to the tunnels to take over from Thorne.

'They killed Agnes,' I told her gently. 'At least she is now beyond anything that our enemies can do to her.'

Thorne did not speak. She simply nodded, but when she passed me to return to the tower, I saw that her eyes were full of tears.

Afterwards I spent a long day down there on watch. Time passed very slowly. At one point I ventured out as far as the small lake that had once been guarded by the wight. But of enemy incursions there was no sign. Perhaps they realized how easy it would be for us to defend the tower. We could kill a lot of them in a confined space such as this. And the kretch would be too big to fit into the tunnel.

However, we could not remain here under siege indefinitely. At some point soon we would have to break out of our confinement and carry the fight to our enemies.

Once again, on returning to the dungeons, I stood beneath the lamias' gibbet and wondered about its purpose, resolving to ask one of them when a suitable moment presented itself.

Soon Slake came down to take my place and I climbed up into the tower again. I had no appetite but ate a few slices of cold meat to help keep up my strength before going out onto the battlements once more.

A gibbous moon filled the clearing with silver light. Everything seemed quiet, but I sniffed a score more witches lurking in the trees, and the kretch was with them. Bowker, the mage, was there too, and soon he walked out into the clearing and looked up towards us. I noticed that he halted only six paces beyond the edge of the trees. He could easily regain their protection before Wynde reached him.

'They said you were brave, Grimalkin! They said you were the greatest witch assassin who has ever lived!' he called, his taunting voice echoing across the clearing. 'But how can that be when you cower within those walls? You are a coward and dare not come forth to face one who is stronger than you. Behold! Here is your death!'

The kretch loped into the clearing like a giant wolf,

jaws wide, its fur a dark shadow against the moon-lit grass. It looked even bigger and more powerful than the last time I had faced it. It halted close to the moat and reared up so that it was balanced on its powerful hind legs. Then its left hand reached into a pouch on its shoulder and drew forth a long thin blade. It no longer had the appearance of a wolf: standing upright, with teeth gleaming and a blade in its hand, it looked daemonic, a creature from a nightmare. And then, to my astonishment, it spoke. I had not guessed that its malevolent creators had given it the power of speech.

'Come and spar with me on the grass if you dare, Grimalkin!' the beast shouted, its voice a deep rumbling growl. 'Let us dance together blade against blade. Join me in the dance of death!'

'One day I will kill you,' I called down. 'But this is not the time. I have other more important things to consider.' I lifted up the leather sack. 'Behold the head of your master! Each night we talk. Each night I teach him about pain. And because of your insolence his torment will increase threefold this night!'

At my words a collective groan went up from the throats of the witches hidden in the forest.

'What about the winged witch at your side?' the kretch snarled, drawing another blade. 'Is she a coward too? She has killed many of us, snatching them from the air, taking advantage of her wings. But dare she face *me* in combat?'

At my side Wynde growled angrily and fluttered her wings.

'Don't listen,' I counselled softly. 'We should save our strength for the right moment.'

'Those words should not go unanswered,' the lamia hissed.

'That's what they are – just words,' I said softly. 'Don't listen. That creature is just trying to provoke us into making a rash attack. "Cowardice" and "courage" are just labels – words invented by foolish men to bolster their egos and denigrate their enemies. In battle we should be cold, clinical and disciplined. That is the way of an assassin and it is what I counsel for you. When the time is right, we will kill the kretch. You will drink its blood and I will take its thumb-bones to wear around my neck.'

'Please, Grimalkin, let me have one of its bones,' Thorne begged.

'We will see, child,' I said, smiling grimly. 'You will receive what you deserve.'

'You whisper amongst yourselves like weaklings!' the kretch called up, pointing its blades towards us. 'You are just frail women who do not deserve the name "witch".'

'I will kill the creature for you, Grimalkin!' Wynde hissed.

'Do not risk it,' I warned. 'It is very fast and strong and its claws contain a deadly poison. Moreover, its bones are as tough as armour. The head is well-protected.'

But then, before I could speak again, Wynde launched herself from the battlements and began to circle the clearing with strong, steady beats of her wings. When she approached the spot where the mage was standing, she banked and swooped towards him, talons outstretched. I thought he would use his mysterious bone weapon against her, but instead he simply stepped back into the trees, and Wynde turned and started to gain height, ready to attack the kretch. I realized that she had simply wanted to drive Bowker out of the clearing so that she could deal with the creature without interference.

The kretch waited, staring up at the lamia, blades ready to meet her. By now Wynde was very high, appearing no larger than a fingernail. Suddenly she dropped like a stone, straight towards her enemy, and everything happened very fast: I saw the blades flash, the lamia strike with her talons, fur and feathers flying everywhere. Then Wynde's wings were unfurled and she was gliding away, gaining height once again.

There were two livid scratches on the kretch's forehead, above its eyes. The lamia had drawn blood, but I knew that the skull beneath the fur was tough. I remembered how it had deflected my throwing knife. I had hurled it accurately and with enough force to penetrate a human skull and bury itself up to the hilt in the brain. The kretch's thick bone had repelled it as easily as would a newly forged helmet, fresh from the anvil of an expert smith. The creature also had rapid powers of recovery. Wynde would have to kill it, then cut it into pieces – and perhaps eat its heart to stop it regenerating.

I glanced up at the lamia as she dived towards the kretch again. She had lost a few wing feathers in that first attack but I knew that her lower body was well protected by scales. In the battle on Pendle my own blades had been powerless, yet my skill as a forger of weapons could only be surpassed by one of the Old Gods, such as Hephaestus. The kretch's weapons would be unable to cut Wynde's belly. It would have to go for something more vulnerable, like the throat. But such a target would be hard to reach, and the creature would have to take risks and increase its own vulnerability.

This time Wynde's attack was slower and she came at the kretch from an angle that was far less steep; maybe something near to forty-five degrees. I saw immediately that she was going for its belly. It saw that, and dropped to all fours and twisted away. It didn't escape completely because the lamia raked its flank with her talons, gouging five long livid wounds. But still they were not serious, and the creature stood up again and waited, blades at the ready. As yet no serious damage had been suffered by either combatant.

I was filled with anxiety for Wynde. What she was attempting was filled with great risk. I wished I could join the fight, but it would take me too long to descend the walls, and only death waited down there. My duty was to keep the Fiend's head safe, not sacrifice myself needlessly.

The lamia's next attack was almost identical to the previous one. That was a mistake because the kretch was ready. This time it dropped onto all fours once more, but as Wynde struck at it with her talons, it rose up and lunged at her throat with its left blade.

Wynde seemed to hesitate, as if uncertain what to do. Then she gave a shudder and took off again. But there was something ponderous about her ascent.

'She's hurt!' Thorne exclaimed. 'She's badly cut.'

Thorne was right. I could see blood dripping from the lamia and spotting the grass. I thought she might retreat back to the battlements. But, like Thorne, Wynde was a taker of risks and she attacked again immediately.

This time she went for the kill. Rather than striking quickly, then flying away to safety, she collided with the kretch with great force, then slashed and tore at it with her talons, fighting at close quarters. She was grasping the creature's shoulder with her right hand, holding it close while she struck at it again and again with the other. But it was striking back, and I could see its blades gleaming in the moonlight, both red with blood as it thrust them into her body. Blood-spattered feathers fell around them and I groaned inside, aware that the lamia was getting the worst of it.

Why didn't she release her hold on her enemy and escape while she still had the strength? Better to retreat and survive to fight another day. Some defeats are temporary. The final victory is all that counts.

And then the bearded mage, Bowker, was running out of the trees towards the combatants, and from a distance of about six paces he pointed his rodent-skull weapon at the lamia: I saw the air shimmer, and Wynde shuddered.

Now it was too late for her to fly to safety. The kretch dragged her down onto the grass beside it; one of her wings was bent at an unnatural angle and I knew that, even had she wished to take off, flight was now beyond her. She fought on for a while and it seemed that the kretch was temporarily baffled and feared the teeth and claws of the lamia.

But then a horde of witches ran out of the forest towards the battle, shrieking with delight, knives at the ready. Three carried long poles to which knives were lashed with rope, and they used these first, stabbing again and again into the vulnerable parts of the lamia while she struggled in the grip of the kretch.

These were witches from the Deane clan. I quickly sniffed out their names: Lisa Dugdale, Jenny Croston and Maggie Lunt. I would not forget this. Soon I would make them pay with their lives.

Wynde shuddered again and again, but she was brave and made no sound despite the agony she was suffering. Thorne and I watched silently from the battlements. I thought of her sister, Slake, guarding the tunnels, unaware of what had befallen Wynde. It was a mercy that she had not witnessed this – she would surely have gone to her sister's aid and died as well.

The witches were in close now, the long-bladed poles no longer necessary because the lamia was immobile – probably already dead. But they took no chances and continued to slice into her body. Moments later we knew why.

The kretch stood up on its hind legs. Its hands no longer wielded blades but they were red with blood. In its left it held the still-beating heart of Wynde. As I watched, it tore it in two and began to eat it, blood staining its teeth and running from its open jaws.

CHAPTER
10
HER SPIRIT LIVES ON

Some worship dark gods; others serve the light,
but I walk alone.
I am Grimalkin.

I watched in silence, powerless, the anger beginning to build within me. The kretch had made certain that the lamia could not return. For Wynde there would be no after-life as a dead witch. She had been sent straight back to the dark.

When it had finished devouring the lamia's heart, the kretch shouted up at us, 'Soon this is what I will do to you! Your days are numbered. Your heart will be mine, Grimalkin. This is the

147

fate that awaits the enemies of my master!'

'For what you have done I will kill you all!' I cried. 'Each and every one of you will die at my hands. Scatter and flee – but I will hunt you to the ends of the earth. I swear it!'

The kretch and the mage simply laughed at my words, and immediately the witches joined in, the cacophony of cackling laughter and wild whoops of amusement echoing across the clearing.

It was time to give them a reply that they would understand, so I bent down, untied the leather sack and drew forth the head of the Fiend. I held it up by the horns so that it was facing out over the battlements.

'Now I will hurt the one whom you most love; the one whom you all serve! This is what your actions have cost your master! He will hold you to account!'

I drew a dagger and plunged it into the right eye of the Fiend, twisting the blade savagely.

The head could not cry out because the mouth was filled with the green apple and rose thorns. But nevertheless there was a terrible scream. It seemed to rise out of the ground beneath our feet. Then a voice boomed out from the bowels of the earth:

'You have failed me! Woe to you all! An eternity of torment awaits those who fail me a second time! What I suffer, you will each suffer a thousandfold!'

The earth trembled, the tower shook, and a vivid streak of forked lightning rent the sky from north to south, the answering rumble of thunder so loud that it drowned out the horrified screams of the witches below. But I could see their mouths open, their eyes filled with horror at what I had done and what the Fiend had said. They ran around in circles like headless chickens while a great wind buffeted the trees, bowing and shaking their branches.

At last calm descended and I looked down at each and every one of the witches in turn so that they could see the death waiting in my eyes.

'Be gone from this place. Go far!' I cried. 'Tomorrow night at this time I will return to the battlements. If I see or sniff your presence in these woods I will put out your master's remaining eye! Do I make myself clear?'

No one answered from below. All were silent – even the bearded mage and the kretch. With bowed heads they turned their backs on me and returned slowly to the cover of the trees.

Thorne was staring at me, her eyes shining. 'You showed them! That shut them up!' she exclaimed.

I nodded grimly. 'But for how long?' I asked.

Black blood was dripping from the ruined eye-socket. I spat on the Fiend's forehead, then returned his ugly head to the leather sack.

'If they stay away tomorrow night, we'll leave this place,' I said.

'Aren't we safer here than anywhere else?' Thorne asked.

'That's not the problem, child. Without the winged lamia to hunt for us we will eventually starve. Not only that – our enemies will gather here in greater and greater numbers. No siege can last for ever.'

She grimaced. 'Where will we go?'

'There are several possibilities, but none of them better fortified than here. Let me think a while. In the meantime we should go down to tell Slake what has befallen her sister.'

We went into the storeroom and passed down through the trapdoor onto the spiral steps and into the damp chill of the lower part of the tower. When we reached the dungeons, I sensed the presence of the lamia. She had already left the tunnels.

We found her kneeling at the foot of the lamia gibbet. The dead animals were still suspended from the chains, but blood no longer dripped into the bucket, which was now full to the brim. Just one torch flickered from a wall-bracket nearby. I sensed no immediate danger. Only a few rats moved in the darkness.

Slake was muttering to herself and swaying rhythmically from side to side. At first I thought that she was weaving a spell, chanting some sort of incantation, but her voice was suddenly filled with fervour, as if she had some desperate need to be heard. She lifted her arms towards the gibbet and bowed three times. Was this some kind of worship? Was she praying to her god? If so, who could it be?

I gestured to Thorne, and we moved back into the shadows beyond the pillars. 'Let her do what she must. We will speak to her when she is ready,' I whispered.

After a few minutes Slake bowed low before rising to her feet. Then she turned to the bucket of animal blood, gave a guttural cry, lifted it to her lips and drank deeply. Three times she cried out, drinking immediately afterwards. By the third cry I realized that it was a word she was calling out – perhaps someone's name.

When the bucket was empty, she replaced it at the foot of the gibbet, turned and approached us. I realized that despite her absorption in what she'd been doing, the lamia had been aware of our presence all along.

Slake bowed to us, though not as deeply as she had before the gibbet. The front of her dress was saturated with blood that had spilled from the bucket. Strangely, her face looked less human than when I had last seen her on the battlements. The eyes were savage, the mouth like a red wound that her own sharp teeth might have devoured from within.

'I'm sorry to bring you bad news,' I said softly, 'but your sister died bravely fighting the kretch. Then the merciless creature ate her heart.'

Not even a flicker of emotion passed across the lamia's face. 'I already know,' she replied. 'I sensed the moment of her death. That is why I was praying.'

'To whom do you pray?' I asked. 'Which god is it?'

'It is the god of all lamias, of course.'

I frowned. 'I do not know of this god.'

'We call her Zenobia She was the first – the ancestor of us all. You were with her in Greece. She is the mother of Thomas Ward, the Spook's apprentice.'

'But she was destroyed fighting the Ordeen.'

Although I was not witness to the event, Tom Ward had told me how his mother in her winged form had held the Ordeen in a death grip. But as they fought, her citadel had been consumed by a pillar of fire and carried back into the dark.

'Not destroyed – her spirit lives on. She has spoken to us. She gave me instructions just then as I prayed.'

I remembered how close Tom Ward had been to his mother. If she had spoken to this lamia, surely she must have communicated with him too?

'Instructions . . . concerning what?' I asked.

'She commanded me to stay here without my sister and defend the tower against our enemies. Above all, I must protect the trunk, which contains information that might aid her son in his attempts to destroy the Fiend.'

'You've already searched that trunk and read the books. What did you learn? Tell me and I will pass it on.'

'It is not straightforward – far from it. Many ages ago Zenobia was in conflict with the Fiend. She tried in vain to destroy him – though she did manage to "hobble" him by means of dark magic, thus placing a limit on his power. These are the terms of that hobble: if he kills Thomas Ward himself, then he'll reign on in our world for a hundred years before he's forced to retreat back to where he came from. But if he enlists the services of one of his children to do the deed – the son or daughter of a witch – then the Fiend can rule on in the world indefinitely. Then there is a third way: if he can convert the boy to the dark, his dominion will also last until the end of the world.

'If we study the manner in which the hobble was imposed we may get an idea of how we can move forward – how the Fiend might finally be destroyed,' Slake continued. 'Zenobia believes that her son might glimpse something that she has missed. There could well be some loophole, a gap into which something new and efficacious may be added.'

I had heard about the hobbles before from Alice Deane. This was the first confirmation that Tom's mother had been responsible. That limitation on the Fiend's power had been vital – otherwise he would have slain Tom Ward years ago. I suspected that the Fiend still hoped to convert the boy to the dark. The apprentice had certainly been moving slowly in that direction, being forced to compromise his beliefs by using the blood jar and allying himself with witches. But I suspected that the Fiend's hatred for Tom and his need for vengeance would drive him to slay the boy the moment he was freed from the binding.

'If you stay here in this tower, how will you survive without food?' Thorne asked.

'I will go hunting for it,' the lamia replied. 'My sister and I hoped to learn what was required and then escape from this refuge in human form and carry the knowledge to the apprentice. Now all has changed. What we seek is beyond our powers of understanding. Very soon the boy must return here and study the books for himself. I have already begun the process that will return me to the feral form. For a few weeks I will have to survive by drinking the blood and eating the flesh of rats, but once my wings are grown I will take to the skies and hunt larger prey – firstly animals, but eventually those who slew my sister.'

I nodded. 'But can you defend the tower alone?'

'It will be hard at first, but I can do it. Later, once I am fully transformed, they will not dare to attack. The kretch is too large to enter the tunnels.'

'Then I think it best that Thorne and I leave while

we can. Besides,' I said with a grim smile, 'I do not share your taste for rats.'

Slake nodded. 'You will leave immediately?'

'No, not until this time tomorrow night. First I will walk the battlements with the head of the Fiend. Immediately after the death of your sister, in revenge I put out one of his eyes with my dagger. If our enemies are nearby, then I will put out the second eye, just as I promised. But they know their master will hold them to account for what he suffers. I expect the wood to be free of witches so that we can travel some distance before being pursued again.'

'Where will we go?' Thorne demanded.

'I think that Clitheroe is probably the best option,' I told her.

'They say it's now a ruined town, full of bandits and cut-throats,' Thorne observed.

'Then what could be a more fitting place?' I answered with a thin smile.

For a long time Clitheroe Castle had held out against the occupying forces. When it had finally fallen, starved out by siege, in revenge the enemy had put the defenders to the sword and burned the town. Now it was a ruin, but the fortification still stood.

The enemy had now been defeated and driven south, but very few of the original inhabitants had returned to Clitheroe to rebuild their homes. Instead it had become a hideout for murderous robbers who pillaged the countryside west of Pendle. No doubt, in time, troops would be sent to put an end to such lawless activities, but in its present state it was just what we needed. We might well be able to get into the castle, seize it from those who occupied it at present and take refuge there.

But first we had to leave Malkin Tower undetected and escape north through the woods.

CHAPTER 11
A GIFT FROM HELL!

A true knight has a strict code of chivalry
by which he lives his life:
he cannot refuse a challenge
and he always keeps his word.
I also have a code of honour,
but it is flexible.

We spent our remaining time in the tower resting to regain our strength for the ordeal ahead, but ate sparingly of the pieces of mutton that Wynde had brought us. Slake would need it more than us; soon she would have to survive on a diet of rats.

While Thorne was guarding the tunnels and Slake was up on the battlements keeping watch, I decided to talk to the Fiend once more. My intention was to exert some pressure on him and make our escape from the tower more certain, so I pulled the head out of the leather sack and placed it on a low table. Then, after I had removed the apple and thorns, I sat down cross-legged before it so that our faces were at the same height.

'If you are able, speak to your servants now. Tell them to go! If they do not leave the wood, I will take your remaining eye.'

'What is evil?' asked the Fiend, disregarding what I had said completely.

'You tell me!' I retorted. 'You are the one who should know!'

The mouth smirked, revealing the stumps of broken teeth. 'The only evil is to deny yourself what you really want,' he replied. 'Thus I do no evil because I always impose my will upon others. I always take what I want!'

'You twist everything,' I accused him. 'No wonder they call you the Father of Lies.'

'What is better – to use one's power to the very limit and test oneself, or to restrain one's natural urges?' he demanded. 'It is better to do the former, to expand and grow in the doing. And what of you, Grimalkin? What is the difference between you and me? That is what you practise too!'

I shook my head. 'I like to test myself and grow in strength and skill, but not at the expense of the weak. You have always hurt others just for the pleasure it gives you. What is the pleasure in that – to hurt those unable to defend themselves?'

'It is the greatest pleasure of all!' cried the Fiend.

There was one question that I had never asked him because I found it very difficult to put into words. But I asked it now, emotion constricting my throat so severely that I barely managed to speak audibly. 'Why did you kill my child?' I demanded, grief threatening to overwhelm me.

'Our child, Grimalkin! *Our* child! I did it because

I could. I also did it to hurt you! I did it because I could not suffer it to live! Grown to manhood, that child would have become my deadly enemy, and a dangerous one too. But now another has replaced him – the boy called Thomas Ward. I will destroy him as well. I cannot allow him to become a man. He must die too, just like your child. Firstly, I will do it because I can! Secondly, to prevent him destroying me. Thirdly, to hurt you, Grimalkin. Because without him your last hope of revenge will be gone!'

Without another word I stuffed the apple and thorns into the ugly mouth and pushed him back into the sack. I was shaking with anger.

Later, Thorne and I both dipped into the books in the large trunk but discovered nothing of any direct use. I did read something written on a single sheet of paper – Tom's mother's account of how she had hobbled the Fiend. But, unlike the faded ink of the other notebooks, this seemed to have been written very recently – surely it could not be her hand?

The Dark Lord wished that I return to his fold and make obeisance to him once more. For a long time I resisted while taking regular counsel from my friends and supporters. Some advised that I bear his child, the means used by witches to be rid of him for ever. But even the thought was abhorrent to me.

At the time I was tormented by a decision that I must soon make. Enemies had seized me, taking me by surprise. I was bound with a silver chain and nailed to a rock so that at dawn the sun's fierce rays would destroy me. I was rescued by a sailor, John Ward, who shielded me from the sun and freed me from the silver chain.

Later we took refuge in my house, and it soon became clear that my rescuer had feelings for me. I was grateful for what he had done, but he was a mere human and I felt no great physical attraction to him. However, when I learned that he was the seventh son of his father, a plan began to take shape within my mind. If I were to bear him sons, the seventh would have special powers when dealing with the dark. Not only that: the child would carry some of my attributes, gifts that would

163

augment his other powers. Thus this child might one day have the ability to destroy the Fiend. It was not easy to decide what to do. Bearing his seventh child might give me the means to finally destroy my enemy. Yet John Ward was just a poor sailor. He came from farming stock. Even if I bought him a farm of his own, I would still have to live that life with him, the stench of the farmyard forever in my nostrils.

My sisters' counsel was that I kill him or give him to them. I refused because I owed him my life. The choice was between turning him out of my house so he could find a ship to take him home, or returning with him.

But to make the second option a possibility, I first had to hobble my enemy, the Fiend. This I did by subterfuge. I arranged a meeting on the Feast of Lammas – just the Fiend and me. After choosing my location carefully, I built a large bonfire and at midnight made the necessary invocation to bring him temporarily into our world.

He appeared right in the midst of the flames, and I bowed to him and made what seemed like obeisance – but

I was already muttering the words of a powerful spell and I had the two sacred objects in my hand.

As I read this account, it seemed to me that Zenobia had hated the Fiend as much as I did and had taken a risk similar to mine when she had summoned him. It had been good to fight beside her in Greece. And now, although no longer clothed in flesh, she was still an entity to be reckoned with. It was gratifying to have her on my side.

    I continued reading:

Despite all his attempts to thwart me, I successfully completed the hobble, paving the way for the next stage of my plan, which began with my voyage to the County and the purchase of a farm.

And so I became the wife of a farmer and bore him six sons, and then, finally, a seventh whom we named Thomas Jason Ward; his first name chosen by his father, the second by me after a hero from my homeland of whom I was once fond.

We lamias are accustomed to shape-shifting, but the changes that time works on us can never be predicted. As the years passed I grew to accept my lot and to love my husband. I moved gradually closer and closer to the light, and eventually became a healer and a midwife, helping my neighbours whenever I could. Thus it was that a human, John Ward, the man who saved me, moved me down a path I had not foreseen.

I could not see how that provided information that might help Thomas Ward to destroy the Fiend, but combined with the other snippets of writing to be found in the trunk, it might tell us something. It was vital that the Spook's apprentice should come and make his own thorough search of the trunk. I resolved to contact Alice again when I got the chance and tell her to bring him to visit the tower once more.

'Who wrote this?' I asked Slake.

'It is in my hand,' she replied. 'It was originally written by Zenobia in code, the text scattered throughout her notebooks. She appeared in a vision to us and granted me the key to unlock this account.'

'What were the sacred objects of which she spoke?'

'One of them is in the trunk,' she replied. 'The other is elsewhere.'

'Where is the other one?'

'I do not know.'

'What is the one in the trunk? Show it to me!' I demanded.

Slake shook her head and regarded me sideways from the corners of her eyes. 'I may not show it to you. Zenobia has dictated that only Thomas Ward may see it.'

I nodded. 'Then guard it well until he can return to this place. You said he must come here soon. How urgent is it?'

'He must visit well before Halloween. Otherwise it may be too late.'

'Our need to destroy the Fiend is indeed urgent,' I replied. 'But why *this* Halloween? What is its significance?'

'There is a cycle of such feasts. The most propitious

occurs every seventeen years. In October it will be thirty-four – twice seventeen – years since Z hobbled the Fiend.'

'So we have until then . . .'

Slake nodded. 'That is all the time that remains.'

But for the problem of the kretch and the other enemies who pursued us, I would have gone directly to Chipenden and brought Tom Ward to the tower to begin his search of the chests. But how could I lead them here and place him in danger?

I must destroy my enemies first. And time was short. It was already late in the month of April.

At last it was time to make our escape north, so I climbed up onto the battlements, carrying the leather sack, flanked by Thorne and Slake. I looked down across the clearing towards the dark line of enclosing trees. There was heavy cloud above and a slight breeze from the west. The poor light would help us to escape unseen. I sniffed quickly three times.

The kretch and the mage were absent, but one

witch remained – perhaps as a spy. I would give her something to report back!

I untied the sack, drew forth the severed head of the Fiend and held it up high, facing towards the spot where I knew the witch to be hiding.

'I smell the blood of a witch!' I cried. 'Did you not heed my warning yesterday? The blame for what I am about to do will fall upon you and *you alone*. Imagine what tortures the Fiend will devise to pay you back for this!'

With these words I drew a dagger and readied it to plunge the blade into the Fiend's remaining eye. There was a cry of distress from the trees, and then the sound of running feet diminishing into the distance.

I smiled and spat on the fiend's forehead again. 'You may keep your second eye for a little while longer,' I said before returning him to the sack.

That done, Thorne and I thanked Slake and took our leave, sensing her sadness. She had shared her sister's life for centuries and was now alone.

We made our escape through the tunnels. There

were no enemies lying in wait at the entrance so we headed north, keeping close to Pendle Hill and passing to the west of Witch Dell. A dead witch only returns to consciousness when the light of the full moon first falls upon her leaf-covered grave. That was still several days away – otherwise I would have entered the dell and paid my respects to Agnes Sowerbutts.

Just south of the village of Downham we turned west and headed downhill towards Clitheroe. There were no lights showing from the town but a fire blazed on the battlements of the castle, confirming that it was occupied.

Suddenly I saw flashes, but they were inside my head, flickering a warning in the corners of my eyes. This time it was about five minutes before the other symptoms began.

I lost my balance, stumbled and fell to my knees. I felt a sharp pain in my chest and I struggled to breathe.

Thorne tried to help me to my feet, but I pushed her away. 'No, child, leave me – it will pass in a moment.'

But it was a long hour before the world stopped

spinning about me and an anxious Thorne was able to help me to my feet again. It would have been better to rest further before entering the ruins of the town but we could not afford the delay. It would not be long before my enemies sniffed the direction I'd taken; soon the kretch would be following our trail once more.

Breathing heavily, I led Thorne down towards the outskirts of the town. The buildings that surrounded the castle were still in darkness but robbers might be lurking there. I came to a halt and knelt on the grass, signalling that Thorne should crouch down beside me.

'I have had heard rumours that Clitheroe is occupied by more than one group,' I told her. 'The strongest band of villains will hold the castle itself, the weaker groups taking what shelter they can amongst the ruins of the town.'

'No doubt they'll be bickering and fighting amongst themselves,' Thorne observed.

'Yes – and that is very much to our advantage as it means that they cannot muster their full force effectively.'

I sniffed the lower reaches of the town for danger and found only sleeping men. We moved cautiously forward past the outlying buildings and into the narrow rubble-strewn streets. Most of the houses were without roofs and the place stank of filth and rot. We began to climb the hill on which the castle stood, picking our way through the streets without being challenged, but at last we came to the high outer stone wall of the fortification. There was no moat and the gate was wide open. Just outside, a man was sitting on a bench beside a brazier of softly glowing coals. He tottered to his feet looking at me in astonishment. Then a bulky figure stepped out of the shadows behind him.

'Look, lads! Women!' the big man cried. 'What a gift from Heaven!'

I opened my mouth and smiled broadly, showing him my pointy teeth.

His face fell. 'There's an old saying – never look a gift horse in the mouth. But it's best to know the truth,' he said, shaking his head in disbelief.

'Yes,' I said softly, 'we are a gift from Hell.'

Thorne moved close to my side and drew two daggers.

'You are mere men! What chance can you possibly have against us?' I jibed, drawing my own blades, hoping to provoke the two bandits into making a reckless attack. I had sensed others hiding nearby also.

The man lifted his heavy spear and pointed it at us, while more men ran to his assistance from the shadows, gathering at his back. They formed a tight bunch behind him and carried an assortment of weapons. Some looked like they had been in the army; they were most likely deserters because the war was still being fought to the south of the County. One even wore a tattered uniform with a red rose epaulette. There were only nine of them, and the big man with the spear was obviously their leader.

'Stay close to me, child, and guard my back,' I whispered into Thorne's ear. 'I'll kill the one with the spear first.'

I ran straight at him. He was big and strong but clumsy, and I parried his spear-thrust with ease. When my blade found his heart, his eyes opened wide in pained astonishment and he collapsed at my feet. Thorne despatched two to my rear while I concentrated on wounding as many of the others as possible. I had killed their leader, and that was enough. I simply wanted to drive them away from the castle. Moments later they had fled, most of them bleeding.

'Now for the battlements,' I said.

We entered the castle and climbed the narrow spiral steps cautiously, alert for danger. The battlements appeared to be deserted but the fire was still burning there, and I could sniff someone's presence – one person: male; young.

Was he waiting in ambush? As we approached the fire, I realized that he was capable of no such thing. He was lying against the wall, gagged and bound from head to foot – a boy of no more than fifteen. I knelt beside him and he flinched as I cut through his bonds, regarding me with wide, terrified eyes.

I returned my blade to its sheath, then pulled him up into a sitting position and took the gag out of his mouth. His face was dirty and covered in bruises, his left eye swollen. But despite that evidence of mistreatment he was good-looking, with blue eyes and fair hair.

'What's your name, boy?' I asked.

He flinched again when I spoke. He was watching my mouth, probably appalled by the sight of my teeth.

I meant the boy no harm, but it gave me satisfaction to see fear in another's eyes. It was a confirmation of who I was. I liked to instil terror and respect.

'W-Will,' he answered, a slight stammer in his voice.

'Well, Will, what did you do to deserve being treated like this?'

'My father is a knight. I was snatched by these bandits, and those escorting me were slain. They're trying to ransom me, but my father can't afford what they are asking. He owns extensive lands, but they are tenanted by many poor farmers and he has little money. Tomorrow they were planning to cut off one of my fingers and send it to him.'

'Your parents must be very upset. It is a terrible thing to abduct a son in this way.'

'My mother passed away three years ago in a plague that swept through the northern lands. But yes, my father loves me very much.'

'Well, you're free to go back to him, boy,' I told him. 'But leaving this stronghold is not a good idea at the moment. There are men down there who would cut your throat as soon as look at you. Where is your home?'

'It's to the north, on the County border. No more than five hours on foot.'

'Does your father know where you are being held captive?'

'He may, but they've told him they'll kill me if he or his men attempt a rescue.'

I nodded, then peered down over the battlements towards the open gate. A group of armed men were gathered just beyond it, looking up towards us. It was time to close the gate and deter any who might be foolish enough to venture in.

'Stay here with the boy, Thorne,' I commanded.

I walked down the steps and crossed the yard, stepping over the bodies of the three we had killed. Words would be wasted on such men. Despite the loss of their leader, no doubt they'd fill themselves with drunken courage and attack before dawn. However, I might be able to frighten them off, so without slowing down, I fingered the bones on my necklace and began to chant the words of a spell under my breath.

It was a pity to use up more of my magical store, because I'd need it later, but it was a spell of illusion and not too costly. Besides, I knew it well and routine makes for economy. It was the spell called *Dread*, and I saw the eyes of the bandits widen and their faces twist with terror. By now, to them, my face would appear daemonic, my hair transformed into writhing snakes with venomous forked tongues.

They had fled before I reached the gate, so I closed it and shrieked at their fast disappearing backs. I had no means to lock it, so I gripped it firmly in both hands and uttered another short spell to bind it shut, at least for a while. I knew it would not withstand the force of the kretch or a band of determined witches. But the former was too big to get up the narrow steps to the battlements, while the latter could be killed one by one as they ascended.

That done, I returned to the castle. I expected the kretch to arrive before dawn.

CHAPTER 12
IT WILL COME TRUE FOR ME

All the prey that I hunt I will eventually slay.
If it is clothed in flesh, I will cut it.
If it breathes, I will stop its breath.

We did not sleep that night and I was ever-vigilant, sniffing the darkness for danger. But we did not go hungry. There were fresh animal carcasses on the battlements, and we roasted half a pig on a spit over the fire, then shared it amongst the three of us. But I was aware that from now on we would have to ration our food and prepare for a siege. At present it was difficult to estimate how long we might have to stay here.

The boy was taciturn, nervous and fearful, but that did not lessen his appetite. While remaining silent, he listened to our conversation with rapt attention – though terror still twitched across his face. His eyes were continually drawn towards the leather bag, which seemed to hold a terrible fascination for him. It may well have been because of the strange sounds that occasionally escaped from it. Despite the large green apple and the rose thorns, the Fiend gave an occasional faint groan or a rustling hiss, as if letting out a breath.

'Well, Thorne,' I demanded. 'In my absence did you continue with your training tasks?'

Thorne smiled at me. 'Every day without fail I repeat the mantra that you taught me. *I am the best, the strongest and the most deadly,*' she said, her voice hardly more than a whisper. 'Eventually I will believe it. It came true for you – one day it will come true for me!'

'Do you still practise with blades every day?' I asked, glancing at Will and delighting in the fear that flickered in his eyes in response to my question.

She nodded, then swallowed a mouthful of pork

before continuing. 'Recently I have been practising throwing my blades. I'm still some years off achieving my maximum strength. Until then, I shall continue to kill my enemies from a distance. When I am taller and heavier, I will move in close! You taught me that too.'

'That's wise. You listen to what I say and act accordingly. I couldn't have wished for better pupil!'

'Your own early training was not so happy,' Thorne remarked, pleased to receive my praise – which I gave only very rarely.

'That's true.'

'Then tell me the tale again. I'm sure Will would like to hear it – wouldn't you?'

The boy nodded, desperate to agree with anything she said.

'Well, then, why don't *you* tell the story for me?' I suggested. 'You've nagged me to the telling often enough – you should know it off by heart by now!'

Thorne shrugged and smiled. 'Why not?' she said, turning to face Will. 'To begin with, I'd better explain that the witch assassin of the Malkin clan is usually chosen by single combat. Challengers must face the incumbent in a fight to the death.

'But first there must be a period of intense training for those who hope to win the right to the position. Grimalkin had decided to become the Malkin witch assassin but came late to that year's preparations. She joined two others who had already been training for six months. What was worse, only half a year remained before the three days assigned for the challenges. So she'd very little time to learn the basics of the assassin's trade.

'Her first day in the training school was a disaster. The other two trainees were weak – doomed to be killed by Kernolde, who was the Malkins' assassin at that time. As the day slowly passed by, Grimalkin became more and more annoyed. At last, just before dark, she voiced her thoughts. She was sitting on the floor looking up at Grist Malkin, their inept trainer, who was blathering on about fighting with blades, his words showing just how ineffectual and stupid he was – he hadn't a clue. Standing behind him were two of the ugliest old hags from our clan, both witches. So ugly were they that they had warts on their warts and more bristles on their chins than on a hedgehog's arse!'

Thorne laughed deep in her throat as she said that, and in response Will gave a weak smile and blushed to the roots of his pale hair.

'The hags were there to make sure the trainees didn't use magic against Grist Malkin,' Thorne continued. 'Her patience finally at an end, Grimalkin rose to her feet and shouted at him.'

I smiled as Thorne lurched to her own feet and shouted out the words as if she were actually there in my place and Will was Grist.

'"You're a fool, Grist! You've already prepared twenty-seven defeated challengers before us. What can you teach us but how to lose and how to die?"'

So vehement was her outburst that Will actually flinched away.

Thorne smiled wickedly. 'You should see Grist now. He retired at the end of that year, and he's grown old and fat. It was this confrontation with Grimalkin that finished him off. For a long time he didn't speak,' she went on, sitting down again, 'but simply locked eyes with Grimalkin and glared, his foolish fat face twitching with fury. He was a bear of a man, at least a head taller than Grimalkin and heavily muscled. But Grimalkin wasn't the slightest bit afraid, and met his gaze calmly. He looked away first. Deep down he was scared, although he tried not to show it.

'"On your feet, child!" Grist commanded. Grimalkin obeyed, but she was smiling and mocking him with her eyes.

'"Take that grin off your face. Don't look at me!" he bellowed. "Look straight ahead. Have some respect for the man who teaches you!" He began to circle Grimalkin slowly. Suddenly he seized her in a bear-hug, squeezing so hard that one of her ribs snapped with a loud pop. Then he threw her down hard into the dirt, thinking that this was the end of the matter.

'But what did Grimalkin do? Did she lie there moaning with pain? No! She was on her feet in an instant and broke his nose with her left fist, the punch knocking him to the ground. And after that she fought like an assassin. You should never let anyone bigger than you get close – she kept him at a distance. The struggle was over quickly. Each blow was well-timed and precise. In moments Grist Malkin was beaten to a pulp! One of his eyes was swollen and closed, and his forehead was split wide open; blood was running into his other eye. Grimalkin punched him to his knees.

'"I could kill you now!" she cried. "But you're just a man and hardly worth the trouble."

'So Grimalkin was forced to train herself. Of course, she was already skilled in forest-craft and forging weapons. So she worked hard, ate well and gradually built up her strength, swimming daily to increase her endurance for fighting – even though it was a long bitter winter, the worst for many a long year. She also forged the best blades she could and carried them in sheaths about her body.

'Then, in a cold northern forest in the dead of winter, she faced a pack of starving wolves. They circled her, moving in slowly, saliva dripping from their jaws, death glittering in their hungry eyes. Grimalkin readied a throwing knife in each hand. When the first wolf leaped, her blade found its throat. The second died just as easily. Finally she drew her long blade as a third wolf bounded towards her. As easily as knocking off a dandelion's head with a stick, she struck the animal's head clean from its body. When the pack finally fled, seven blood-splattered bodies lay dead, staining the white snow red.

'At last it was time for Grimalkin to face Kernolde and she returned to Pendle. Kernolde slew the first two challengers easily enough – in less than an hour, without breaking a sweat. Finally it was Grimalkin's turn—'

'If you are so strong and brave, why have you taken refuge in this castle?' Will interrupted. 'I think my father is braver than either of you!'

We both stared at the boy in surprise. Out of the corner of my eye, I noted the anger that flickered across Thorne's face. I put my hand on her shoulder to restrain her. Then I answered the boy.

'Of course your father is brave,' I agreed, smiling without opening my mouth – for what son would not think that of a father who was good to him? 'He is a knight and it must be part of his nature. Do minstrels sing his praises?'

'They do! He has fought and overcome many opponents, but his greatest deed was to slay the Great Worme that besieged our castle.'

'Are wormes real?' Thorne asked. 'I thought they were just stories told at dusk to scare children.'

'They are indeed,' I replied. 'Wormes are dangerous creatures covered in tough scales and have jaws filled with powerful fangs. Many have long snake-like tails, which they use to wrap around their victims and squeeze the life from them. They usually drain the blood of cattle but like to eat humans whole – blood, flesh and bones. They are quite rare in the County,' I continued, 'and I have seen only one. It was lurking in long grass on the edge of a lake: I was curious and wanted a closer look. As I approached, it slid into the water and quickly swam away. It was no larger than a dog.'

But some wormes could be bigger, or so I had heard. 'You called it the *Great* Worme – was it exceptionally large?' I asked the boy.

'It was the biggest anyone had ever seen – much bigger than a horse. My father had a special suit of armour forged – one covered with sharp metal spikes. When the worme wrapped itself around him, its body was pierced and he cut it to pieces with his sword.'

I smiled, showing him my teeth. Once more he flinched. 'You said that your father is a knight without wealth. How many men does he have at his disposal?'

'He has few men, but those he commands are well-trained – including eight master archers skilled with the longbow.'

I liked what I was hearing. I realized that this knight with his spiked armour and expert bowmen might make the killing of the kretch far easier.

'Listen, boy,' I told Will. 'I too am brave, and so is Thorne. We have taken refuge in this fortification because we are being pursued by many powerful enemies. That alone would not dissuade me from facing them directly in combat, but by dark magic they have created a terrible creature which is part wolf and part man. Until I find a way to destroy it I need a refuge such as this. But I think your father's castle would be a better place. Not only that – your brave father and his archers could help me to destroy my enemies. If I help you to escape this place and deliver you safely to him, would he give us shelter in his castle, do you think? Would he put his fighting prowess next to ours and help us to victory?'

'I'm sure he would!' Will cried out, his eyes shining. 'Get me to safety and I promise that he will help you!'

I turned to face Thorne. 'We came here out of desperation. We will be hard pressed to defend this castle – the Fiend's servants may lay siege for weeks and starve us out. Now we have the chance of a proper refuge. The journey will be risky, but once we reach it we will be far safer than we are here. What do you say?'

Thorne assented, so I turned back to face the boy, staring hard into his eyes. 'Even if we rescue you, we are still witches, feared and loathed by many people, especially men, and we cannot be sure that your father will honour the promises of his son.'

'I give you *my* word,' he replied. 'My father is a man of honour; he will be *bound* by what I have promised.'

I thought quickly. Could the boy really hold his father to that promise? It was possible. Knights – like all men – varied in their characters: some were good, others bad, while most balanced on a line between the two states. However, many did hold to a code of chivalry. Above all, they believed in honour and kept their word. I looked down at the gate. Soon the kretch would arrive. Despite my magic it would eventually tear the barrier from its hinges and then the Fiend's human servants would attack. We would hold them off at first, but how many more would come, summoned from the far corners of the world to take back the head? In the end we would lose.

I dozed for a while, leaving Thorne on watch. I awoke to the murmur of voices and slowly opened one eye.

Thorne and the boy were sitting very close together,

almost touching, and talking together softly in an animated way, lost in their own private world. It was the first time I had ever seen Thorne show interest in a boy, but she had reached an age when the right one might hold a fascination for her. They clearly liked each other, and it put me in mind of my first meeting with the Fiend.

I was young, not much more than sixteen, when I first encountered him. Of course, I did not know he was the Fiend. I was passing a ruined chapel – one abandoned by the Church after the local population had dwindled; the bishop had deconsecrated the ground ten years earlier and it was now a wilderness of empty graves.

A young man was standing in the shadows watching me. I was annoyed to find myself being stared at and I prepared to cast a small spell – nothing too severe; one that would have loosened his bowels rather suddenly or brought vomit up into his throat. But then he did something that pushed all such thoughts from my mind.

He smiled at me.

Never had I been smiled at in such a way, with such warmth and evident liking. He was handsome too, and tall – I have always liked tall men – and before the night was done we had kissed and lain snugly in each other's arms.

It was Agnes Sowerbutts who put me wise. I had been in the company of the Devil! she told me. At first I found it hard to believe. Surely he could not be the Fiend! How could this beautiful, kind young man be reconciled with the fearsome beast who appeared in the flames of the bone-fire at Halloween? And how could I have been such a fool and fallen so easily for his charms? I was both annoyed and disgusted with myself – I had a bitter hatred of the Fiend and didn't want to believe what Agnes had told me.

But once I'd finally accepted the truth, I knew what to do: bear his child and I could be free of him for ever.

I looked at Thorne, talking happily to her new friend. She did not know I was watching her – otherwise she would not have sat so close to him.

Foolish child, don't you know that most men are devils inside?

But I did not speak the words aloud. We must snatch happiness where we can. I would not begrudge her a few sweet moments.

The clouds had cleared, and to the east the sky was rapidly growing lighter. The sun would be up soon. Better to leave now under cover of what little darkness remained.

'Right, boy – in return for what you have promised, we will take you to your father's castle!' I announced suddenly.

Both Thorne and Will flinched at my unexpected interruption of their cosy chat. They were startled, and quickly, almost guiltily, drew away from each other.

We rose to our feet and I stared at the boy hard, and once more showed him my teeth. 'At all times take up a position between us and obey everything I say without question. Is that understood?'

Will nodded and, hefting the leather sack up onto

193

my shoulder, I led the way down the steps, Thorne bringing up the rear. We ran directly across the yard to the gate. I uttered the words to disable the spell and pulled it open. Were we being watched? I sniffed quickly, and my nostrils were assaulted by waves of fear, drunkenness and growing bravado. The bandits were not yet ready to attack. They were too busy getting drunk to watch the gate.

I sprinted north down the hill with the others following. Soon we were within the labyrinth of dark narrow streets. Mostly they were deserted, but on one corner a drunkard stepped into our path, his mouth opening in surprise. I pushed him hard and he fell back into a doorway while we ran on.

And then I smelled it.

It was the unmistakable stink of the kretch. It had already entered the town.

CHAPTER
13
IN THE COMPANY OF WITCHES

He who eats with the Devil needs a long spoon.
He who walks with a witch
should also keep his distance.

I came to a halt and sniffed again. The creature was approaching from the south and was on our trail.

Thorne sniffed, then smiled. 'The bandits are between us and our enemies. That should prove interesting! They'll be wetting themselves!'

We ran on, and soon we heard a distant bestial roar, followed by screams and shouts of fear and anger. The drunken men would stand no chance against our enemies, but they might slow up the pursuit a little. I glanced back at the boy; he was breathing heavily with the exertion of the run. Whatever his level of fitness, his confinement would have weakened him.

I halted again, handed the sack to Thorne and grabbed the boy. He flinched at my close proximity but did not resist as I hoisted him up onto my shoulder. We continued north at a slightly slower pace. My weakness had not returned, but my stamina was not as good as usual. I tried to put all doubts about my fitness to the back of my mind, but they nagged at me like rotting teeth. I pushed them away and tried to be optimistic. So far my bouts of weakness had not occurred at moments of immediate danger. Despite Agnes's concerns that my body might be permanently damaged, I still hoped to make a full recovery.

By late morning we had slowed our pace to a fast walk. We seemed to have left the kretch behind, though without doubt it still followed us. Now a threat lay ahead. We were following a dirt track through a narrow treeless valley with low hills on either side. Twice I had glimpsed figures on the skyline. We were being watched.

I halted and eased Will back onto his feet. 'How far to the castle now, boy?' I asked.

'Less than an hour. My father's men already provide an escort,' he said, gesturing up to the summits of the hills.

'I've seen them already,' I told him. 'No doubt they will already have sent word that you are in the company of witches.'

Ten minutes later we saw dust on the horizon directly ahead. It was a man on horseback, galloping straight towards us. I sniffed concern but little fear.

'It's my father!' Will exclaimed as the rider drew closer.

The knight wore light chain mail and was mounted on a dappled mare. He had no helmet but carried a sword at his hip and a shield slung across his shoulder. He halted his horse in front of us, barring our path, and drew his sword, pointing it right at us.

'Stand back and allow my son to step forward!' he commanded.

The knight was of middle age and, to my judgement, slightly overweight. He was no real threat to either me or Thorne. No doubt he had declined physically since the deeds of his younger days, but he still had courage. Not many men would dare face two witches with a mere sword.

'He is free to do as he pleases,' I answered. 'Lower your sword!'

'Do not attempt to command me, witch!' he retorted.

'But they freed me, Father, and helped me to escape from my captors,' Will interceded. 'They are pursued and I have offered them refuge in our home. I said that you would help them to fight the dangerous enemies that are on their tail. I gave my word.'

Anger flickered across the knight's face. I sensed that he was a fair man but he seemed less than pleased by what his son had agreed.

'I thank you for freeing my son,' he answered,

lowering his sword and returning it to its scabbard. 'For that I am in your debt. But this presents me with no small difficulty. I am a God-fearing man; within my castle is a chapel where the faithful worship every Sunday. The bishop himself visits twice a year to bless the altar and pray for the sick. My chaplain will be outraged.'

'My word of honour, Father!' Will cried, his voice becoming shrill. 'I gave them my word!'

The knight nodded. 'What's done is done. I will ride on with my son. My home lies directly ahead. Its gates will open for you. I am Sir Gilbert Martin. How are you named?'

'I am Grimalkin and this is Thorne,' I told him. I saw fear in his face and was pleased to note that my notoriety had preceded me. I wanted him to be afraid because then he was more likely to be cooperative.

'Go with your father, boy,' I said, turning to Will. 'We will join you soon.'

With that, the boy ran forward, and his father leaned down, grabbed his arm and helped him up onto the horse behind him. Then, without further acknowledgement, they galloped away into the distance.

'Do you think he will let us into his castle?' Thorne asked.

I shrugged. 'I have my doubts. Soon we will know what honour is worth to such a man. But I think that what waits ahead is better than what follows behind.'

So we continued along the dusty track until the castle came into view; before it ran a narrow fast-flowing river. The fortification was modest, with just a single inner keep, but it did have a moat and a draw-bridge, above which stood a small defensive tower with battlements. Surrounding the castle lay the cultivated fields of tenant farmers, dotted with small cottages, but there was no one working there. I noted that two of the dwellings were burned and blackened. The war had reached even this isolated backwater of the County.

We crossed the river at a ford, the water reaching up to our knees. As we passed the first cottage, I peered through the window to confirm what I had suspected.

I was right: a half-eaten meal lay on the table. The

occupants had left in a hurry. In times of danger the tenants, workers and servants of a knight such as this took refuge within the castle. But what did the knight consider the danger to be? Did he fear two witches or that which pursued them? Perhaps both? We would find out soon enough.

As we got nearer, I saw figures watching us from the ramparts. There was a clank and grinding of chains over a capstan and the drawbridge was slowly lowered, but when we stepped onto it, we saw that the portcullis and the sturdy iron-studded door beyond it were still closed against us.

Then a voice called down to us from above. It wasn't the knight – just one of his minions. I sniffed and knew him for a blusterer – but one who could kill in cold blood and made his living by use of violence.

'Unsheath your weapons! Place them at your feet!' he cried.

I shook my head. 'My blades stay where I can reach them!'

I sniffed again and found danger. There were armed

men in a state of high alert. But I sensed discipline too. They were obedient and awaiting orders.

There was no reply, but I heard murmurs from above. My refusal was being debated.

Seconds later there was a clank of chains and the portcullis began to rise. Thorne leaned across and whispered in my ear. 'It could be a trap,' she said.

I nodded but did not reply. Could we trust this knight? I wondered. I sniffed – this time a long-sniff, attempting to read the future, especially the threat of death. I sniffed for Thorne. She would not die here. I felt sure of it.

The heavy wooden door swung inwards, groaning on its hinges. About ten paces beyond the door stood the knight; behind me there was another closed portcullis. He was still dressed in chain mail but no longer carried the sword. He beckoned us forward, and Thorne and I stepped through the doorway, advancing about five paces. As we came to a halt, the portcullis behind us started to descend. I glanced back and saw that the inner door remained open.

'You are welcome to my home,' Sir Gilbert said, his voice mild and courteous. 'I bear no arms within these walls and I ask that you do likewise. Remove your blades and lay them at your feet.'

'Your customs are not my customs,' I replied. 'My habit is to keep my blades within reach at all times.'

'I offer you refuge but it must be on my terms!'

I drew a throwing blade and pointed it towards him. No sooner had I made that threat than two bowmen moved into position behind him, their arrows pointing through the bars of the portcullis. I glanced to my left and right. There were arrow-slits in the stone walls. We were being targeted from three sides. Arrows fired from longbows had great velocity and force. They could even puncture armour. But despite the extreme danger I remained very calm as I analysed the situation and considered my options.

'Before an arrow reaches me,' I threatened, 'my blade will be in your throat.'

That was true. To slay the knight would be as easy

as flicking a fly from my brow. He was less than a second from death. We could also slay the bowmen behind him. I could not be sure of killing the men behind the arrow-slits though. And even if I was successful, we would be trapped in this gateway with a portcullis on either side and no means of escape.

'Then all three of us would be dead,' said the knight. 'It would be a waste, and so unnecessary. You rescued my son, and for that I am grateful and will hold to his word. I offer you refuge within these walls. Food, drink and clean clothes await you. Just put down your weapons, I beg you, and all will be well.'

Our eyes met and I read his intent – he meant every word – so in answer I knelt and began to take out my blades and lay them down on the floor. After a moment's hesitation, Thorne did likewise. When I returned to my feet, Sir Gilbert was smiling.

'Is that all?' he enquired. 'Have I your word that there are no weapons in the bag on your shoulder?'

'It contains no weapons – I give you my word,' I replied.

'What does it contain?'

'Something that must remain in my presence at all times. If you like I will show it to you later. But then you will wish you had never seen it.'

The knight raised his hand and the bowmen behind the inner portcullis stepped to one side; it began to rise. He gestured for us to follow him and we stepped through into the castle yard. To the left, in the wide area furthest from the inner tower, the estate workers were gathered with their families, cooking over braziers. They were accompanied by sheep, cows and goats; they had evidently brought all their livestock within the walls for safety.

There were few soldiers to be seen, but the eight archers remained by the gate, arrows now returned to their quivers. Then I noticed a figure in the distance: he was garbed in the black cassock of a priest and was frowning as he stared towards us. He was someone who would certainly not greet us with open arms.

We followed Sir Gilbert into the inner tower. A female servant waited just within the entrance. She was matronly, getting on in years, and was dressed in a grey smock with mousy hair pulled back into a tight bun.

'This is Mathilde,' said the knight. 'She will take you to your room. When you are washed and dressed appropriately, she will bring you to the banqueting hall.'

With those words, he smiled, bowed and left us.

'This way, please,' Mathilde said, scurrying off down a corridor. I noticed that she avoided our gaze, no doubt fearing the evil eye. She opened the door to our quarters and left hurriedly.

Thorne's eyes opened wide in amazement at the opulence of our surroundings; she had known nothing before this but witches' hovels and the dwellings of the poor. The room was large and hung with tapestries which seemed to tell a story: a knight was fighting a huge fanged creature in the middle of a fast-flowing river. No doubt it was Sir Gilbert defeating the worme. I quickly glanced about me: there were two beds, two upright chairs and a table bearing a large pitcher of water. On each bed was draped a pale-green dress.

'Dressed appropriately!' I said, raising my eyebrows and smiling at Thorne. 'Have you ever worn a dress such as that before?'

Thorne shook her head. She wasn't smiling. 'We have given up our weapons and now must dress like foolish women of the court. There are no bowmen here to enforce Sir Gilbert's will. Why should we obey?'

'It will do no harm, child, to see how others live. We should wash the stink from our bodies and dress in clean clothes for a while. Soon the kretch will arrive, so enjoy this brief respite. In any case, no doubt the boy will approve of the dress!'

Thorne blushed to the roots of her hair but was too embarrassed to make any reply, so I turned away and laid my straps and sheaths down beside the bed. I took off my dirty clothes and washed myself while Thorne sulked. That done, I donned what seemed to be the longer of the two dresses. When I'd finished, Thorne grudgingly began her own ablutions. At last she faced me, wearing her green dress.

'What a pretty lady you are,' I mocked, 'and more than ready to take your place at court!'

Thorne's face twisted in fury and she ran at me, nails ready to rip my face off.

I took a step backwards and smiled, holding out my hand to ward her off. 'I'm only jesting, child. Don't take offence. Wear your best smile so that we can charm this knight and bend him to our will.'

When we left the room, Mathilde was waiting nervously in the corridor; she led us straight to the banqueting hall. She glanced at the leather bag, which I carried in my left hand. I saw her shudder. Maybe she sensed the evil within. Some people were sensitive to such things.

The hall was huge, with a high hammer-beam roof, and could probably have accommodated a hundred people. There were six long tables, with an oval one at the head, opposite the main door. This was the only one occupied. Two people were seated there: Sir Gilbert and his son. They were finely dressed in dark blue silk, as befitted gentlemen of a court. However, the father would have looked better in his chain mail – his round belly was now open to our gaze: he was clearly a man grown comfortable in middle age and accustomed to an easy life.

As we approached, they both rose to their feet and smiled, but I noticed their gaze flick towards the leather bag, which I placed beside my chair. I wondered where the kretch and the other supporters of the Fiend were now. They might arrive at the castle at any time.

'You are welcome. Be seated,' Sir Gilbert said; he and his son waited until Thorne and I had both taken our places before they sat down.

Servants moved in and placed dishes of meat and bread on the table.

'We have much to discuss, but you must be hungry. So let's eat first and talk later.'

I needed no second invitation. While we ate, large glasses of mead were poured, but both Thorne and I sipped sparingly. We needed clear heads to negotiate with this knight. He had given us refuge – but for how long? There was still much to be decided.

When we had finished, the servants collected the plates but left the glasses before us. Sir Gilbert steepled his fingers and looked at each of us in turn before speaking. 'Once again I must thank you for rescuing my son and escorting him home. He tells me that you are being pursued by some strange creature which is unknown to me. I would know more.'

'The creature is called a kretch, and is a hybrid of a man and a wolf: it has been created by dark magic specifically to hunt me down. It is intelligent and ferocious, and possesses great strength. It can use weapons such as blades, and its claws are coated with a deadly poison. Additionally its head and upper body are armoured with thick ridges of bone and if wounded, it can regenerate itself.'

'How could it be killed?' he asked.

'It is possible that removing the heart and destroying it by fire or eating it might suffice. But in order to be sure, it needs to be dismembered and cut into small pieces.'

'It is not alone?'

'It is accompanied by a band of witches and a

powerful dark mage named Bowker. Their combined strength makes them formidable.'

'And what have you done to make them hunt you down in such a way?'

I reached down and lifted the sack onto the table. 'Within this sack is the head of the Fiend,' I said. 'He has been bound temporarily while we search for a way to destroy him. Our enemies wish to reunite the head with the body and set him at liberty.'

'I find this hard to believe,' said the knight, an expression of incredulity on his face. 'You mean the head of the Devil himself is within that sack? Is that what you are telling me?'

'He was summoned to earth by the Pendle covens. Now he is trapped in the flesh and in great pain. Do you not believe me? Do you require proof?' I demanded.

A faint groan issued from the sack, and what sounded like a sharp intake of breath. Will and his father both started, but the latter quickly regained his composure.

'I am a man of peace and happy attending to my own affairs. I take up arms only when the cause justifies it. I know little of witches and dark magic and believe that much that seems strange can be put down to superstition and ignorance. But I do have an open mind and would very much like to see the contents of this sack.'

'Then I will grant your wish,' I said, undoing the ties. I lifted the Fiend's head out by its horns and held it up before the knight and his son.

Both came to their feet in shock. The boy looked as if he was about to flee from the chamber. The head groaned faintly once more, and the flesh around the ruined eye twitched. There was a thick crusting of blood running from that eye to the wide-open mouth. If anything, the head was even more hideous than before.

CHAPTER
14
ATTACK!

Your magic daunts me not,
because I have magic of my own.
And boggarts, ghosts and ghasts
are no greater threat to me
than they are to a spook.

'It still lives! How can this be?' asked Sir Gilbert, whose face was suddenly very pale.

'Flesh is just a covering,' I replied. 'For the Fiend, the form he takes is just like slipping into a garment. He can assume many such shapes, and his spirit can survive extreme mutilation; it now dwells within the two halves of his body. Thus he must remain trapped.

If his servants return his head to his bound body, he will be free and his vengeance will be terrible, both in this life and beyond.

'Recently he walked the earth and things became darker than at any time in living memory. One manifestation of this was the war that has visited the County, bringing with it death, starvation and cruelty. The fact that he is temporarily bound has already improved matters. *Keeping* him bound is in your interests too.'

Sir Gilbert stared at the Fiend's head. 'Return that fearful thing to the sack, I beg you. It's not a sight that mortal eyes should gaze upon.'

I did as he requested and the four of us sat down again.

'Did you fight in the war?' I asked.

The knight shook his head. 'I am no longer a young man and was not called upon to do so. I stayed behind and tried to protect my people. We were lucky, and being somewhat isolated were visited by only one patrol, and that somewhat late in the campaign. At first my people took refuge in the castle, but when the enemy soldiers started to burn their cottages, I sallied forth at the head of a small but determined force. We lost two of our number but killed every last one of the enemy – eleven are buried in unmarked graves. Thus none escaped to make report.'

'Do we have a good stock of provisions?' I asked.

'Within these walls there are many mouths to feed, but we could endure a siege of several weeks before we began to starve. However, it would not be pleasant and would cause serious difficulties once life returned to normal. Fodder for the cattle is limited and we would have to start slaughtering them. The aftermath of war would make restocking difficult.'

'I think we could finish it relatively swiftly,' I told him. The plan had been forming in my head on the journey to the castle, and now I put it into words. 'With your help we could take the battle to our enemies. Some of them are witches, but your son says that your archers are masters of their trade, and dark magic surely won't be able deflect all their arrows. As for the kretch, you may just be able to attend to it yourself – in the same way that you slew the Great Worme.'

Will smiled, his face glowing with pride. 'Look at the tapestries that adorn your room,' he said. 'They tell the story of what happened fifteen years ago. It shows my father slaying the Great Worme that had devastated the surrounding countryside. What he achieved once, he may do again, employing the same means.'

Thorne turned towards Will and smiled too. When their eyes met, I could see that a bond was forming between them.

The father nodded, but I suspected he was somewhat less enthusiastic about the idea than his son.

It was after dark when Thorne and I returned to our room. Candles were flickering in their holders beside our beds. I picked one up and carried it across to the first of the tapestries; there were five in all.

The worme was depicted laying waste to farmland – carcasses of sheep lay scattered about a field. It held a man in its jaws, only his legs visible. The worme depicted was huge. I had never heard tell of one so big. No doubt the embroiderer had exaggerated its size for effect.

In the second tapestry the worme was advancing upon the castle and the knight was riding out to meet it. The river lay between them. In the third, he had dismounted and was walking into the water at the ford in full armour; the worme was surging towards him, jaws wide open.

The fourth tapestry showed them locked in combat, and the manner of the knight's eventual victory was now clear. The battling figures filled the whole tapestry, and I could see that Sir Gilbert's armour was covered in spikes. The worme had wrapped its body and tail tightly around him, and was being pierced by the spikes and cut to pieces, bleeding in a dozen different places as the knight sliced into it with his sword, which he wielded two-handed. In the final tapestry, Sir Gilbert was holding the head of the creature aloft in triumph, and pieces of it were being carried downstream by the torrent.

'Could he really deal with the kretch in the same manner?' asked Thorne.

'Perhaps, child. It might be worth a try. If we and some of the knight's men engage the others, his protective armour might just enable him to cut it into pieces. Under pressure from his son he seems prepared to try, and I am inclined to encourage that endeavour.'

Our enemies arrived early in the morning of the following day – about twenty of them, accompanied by the kretch and Bowker. They didn't cross the river but, after staring towards the castle for a while, settled down beside the largest of the outlying farmhouses and lit cooking fires.

All through the afternoon they kept their distance while we watched from the battlements. But new bands of witches were arriving by the hour. By evening I estimated that our enemy numbered over a hundred. In addition to the external threat, tensions were rising within in the castle.

'It's the priest. I saw him over there, stirring up trouble,' Thorne said, pointing to where the farmers were camped by their animals. 'I was standing by the gate and he kept pointing at me.'

'He is a priest, child, so it is only to be expected. And those people have been forced to take refuge within these walls because of us. There is bound to be resentment.'

We dined with the knight and his son again that evening, and Thorne told our host about the priest.

'You need not concern yourself about him,' Sir Gilbert replied. 'Father Hewitt has already been to see me and asked that I banish you from the castle. I refused, and the matter is closed. He is my chaplain and has been with us for many years. Indeed, were I to die before my time, he would become the guardian of my son until he reaches maturity. But he is a priest and you are witches so there is a natural enmity between you. There is little he can do but stir up the feelings of his flock. But I am their lord and they will obey me in all things. You are perfectly safe here.'

'We are grateful for that,' I told him. 'I examined the tapestry in our room with interest. I assume that you still have that armour?'

'I do indeed. I had it specially made and it proved most effective against the worme. In truth, the creature was not quite as large as the embroidery suggests,' he said with a smile. 'But it was a dangerous beast and killed many humans as well as cattle.'

'Father is both clever and brave,' Will stated proudly. 'Minstrels still sing of what he achieved.'

'You must be very proud of your father,' I said, smiling at the boy. But then I turned back to Sir Gilbert. 'Such armour may not be as effective against the kretch. It has bone-armour of its own. If we engage it, we should work as a team and we should do it soon, before too many more of the Fiend's servants arrive. Their numbers will grow by the day. But destroy the kretch and we will leave this place and they will follow. You will be able to return to the routine of your lives.'

'We will do it tomorrow, then,' said the knight. 'We

need to find some way to lure them closer to the castle, within range of my archers.'

I nodded. 'I will think of something. And tomorrow we will put an end to them. You will return our blades?'

'Of course. We will leave the castle together with the weapons necessary for victory.'

But I was wrong, and events did not turn out as I had expected.

CHAPTER 15
A FIGHT TO THE DEATH

It is better to fight than to be a mere spectator.
A witch assassin craves combat.

We had a pre-dawn breakfast and then, to Thorne's relief, we put aside the green dresses and once more attired ourselves as assassins. I was looking forward to the coming battle and felt comfortable to be dressed once more in the garb of my calling.

I could not risk taking the Fiend's head with me into battle so it had to be hidden. I used more of my precious remaining magic to achieve that. Using many cotton threads which I unpicked from the hem of my dress, I hung the leather sack from a ceiling beam in the darkest corner of the room. Once that was done, I cloaked it thoroughly. Only a powerful witch or mage could find it now; even for them it would not be easy.

Sir Gilbert, dressed in his spiked armour, was waiting for us in the courtyard, surrounded by his men. So were our blades. It was a good feeling to slip each one back into its scabbard.

It was a grey, misty morning and the air was chilly and damp. I looked at our small war band and gauged our chances of victory. The men looked confident and well-disciplined. In addition to the knight in his deadly armour, there were the eight master archers and another fifteen men-at-arms. All were on foot. Sir Gilbert had told me that they would not put their horses at risk. We were heavily outnumbered but had a good chance of achieving a temporary victory.

I had outlined my plan to the knight and he had given it his approval. The intention was to destroy the kretch and kill as many witches as possible before retreating back into the castle. Later, under cover of darkness, Thorne and I would make our escape; the surviving witches would follow, leaving the inhabitants of the castle and its surroundings to return to their peaceful lives.

But then things started to go wrong. A soldier on watch on the battlements called a warning down to us. The enemy were approaching.

From that high vantage point I estimated their number. There were indeed well over a hundred, led by the kretch and the dark mage. They halted about two hundred yards short of the moat, and the kretch came forward alone. Once directly below us, it rose up on its hind legs, drew a blade and called out a challenge in its booming voice.

My heart sank. The challenge was not aimed at me, but at the knight.

'Sir Gilbert Martin, I hail thee! You are the slayer of the Great Worme and famed throughout this land for what you have achieved. I wish to pit myself in personal combat against one of such renown. Defeat me, and those with me will disperse and trouble you no more.'

'If I lose the fight, what then?' the knight called down. 'I would know the terms of combat.'

'Defeat will cost you your life and the siege will continue. That is all. Do you accept my challenge?'

'I accept, and will fight you in single combat before these walls. Do you agree? Do I have your word?'

'You have my word. We will fight at the water's edge where you defeated the Great Worme. Your followers must remain within the castle walls. My people will retreat far beyond the river.'

'It is agreed!' Sir Gilbert replied.

With that, the kretch bowed its head slightly, showed its teeth in a wicked grin and turned to lope back towards the river.

I almost called down my own challenge to the kretch, but the knight had given his word: I could not intervene. However, I did make an attempt to dissuade him.

'It's a trick!' I warned. 'Such a creature does not think like you. Neither do its companions. They are the servants of the Fiend – the Father of Lies. They have no idea of honour. Go down there alone and you will die! They want the head of the Fiend and have no intention of dispersing until it is in their possession.'

'That may be so,' Sir Gilbert said, turning to face me. 'But as a knight I am not at liberty to refuse a challenge to single combat. It is the code by which I live. And even if that creature does intend to deceive me, all is not lost. When I leave, close the main gate but do not lock it. Leave the drawbridge down too. At the first sign of treachery come to my aid. There is little difference in this to what we intended.'

'I cannot agree,' I warned. 'We would have left this place as a compact unit and protected your flanks and rear as you attacked the kretch. Now you will fight alone and at some distance from us. If there is treachery, we may not be able to come to your aid in time.'

He bowed his head in acknowledgement of what I had said, but he remained resolute, and without another word went down to await the opening of the gate and the lowering of the drawbridge.

When this was done, Sir Gilbert clasped hands with

his son in a brief farewell. Will looked very proud of his father, but his bottom lip was trembling with emotion and I knew that he feared for him. The knight lowered the visor on his helmet and strode towards the river. The door was closed after him but not locked. The archers and men-at-arms waited behind it, weapons at the ready. But I led Thorne back up onto the battlements, where we would get a better view of the fight.

Sir Gilbert was approaching the river ford, and I could see the kretch waiting on the far bank. Of the mage and witches there was no sign, but a wall of thick mist had appeared about a hundred yards away covering both banks of the river. No doubt it had been conjured by magic: they could easily be hiding within it – much closer to the combatants than we were. I sniffed, and immediately sensed danger. It was a trap – I was certain of it. But what could I do? I had warned the knight but he had not heeded my words.

No sooner had he left the muddy bank and entered the shallow water of the ford than the kretch loped towards him, running on four legs like a giant wolf, sending up a curtain of water. Sir Gilbert had not anticipated its speed and he drew his sword too late. The huge beast clamped its jaws upon his right, sword arm and bit hard. Even at that distance I heard the knight cry out in pain.

And what of the kretch? There were spikes on the metal plates that enclosed Sir Gilbert's arm. Now they must surely be cutting into the creature's jaws. It had gradually been changing and growing more powerful. Was it now impervious to pain? Or able to overcome it and exert its will despite the agony it must be feeling? That made it very dangerous indeed. Only death would stop it.

With a great effort, the knight tore his arm free. As he did so, blood dripped from the open jaws of the beast, staining the water. There was blood on the armour too, but was it Sir Gilbert's blood or the beast's?

Even from this distance I could see that the metal covering the knight's arms was dented, and he struggled to lift the sword as the kretch attacked again.

The creature seemed even larger, and it reared up to tower over him. It was growing more powerful with each day that passed.

Although hurt, Sir Gilbert was brave and did not flinch but stood his ground, transferring the sword to his other hand. The weapon was heavy and should really have been wielded with both hands. Nevertheless with his left hand – no doubt the weaker of the two – he thrust the point into the creature's belly. This time it did feel pain and let out a shrill scream, immediately followed by a bellow of anger.

The scream made me feel a lot better. The kretch could be hurt. Yes, I wanted the knight to put an end to it, but really I longed to slay it myself. It was a long time since I'd wanted to hurt and kill something so much. And yet I could not venture forth while the knight was still standing his ground. He was a brave man and I would not deny him his chance of victory.

Knight and kretch came together hard; locked in battle, they fell into the shallow water and rolled over and over until they reached the far bank where they continued to struggle in the mud. This was exactly what Sir Gilbert wanted: now the beast was being impaled on the spikes, hopefully to suffer the same fate as the worme. But as they thrashed about, it seemed to me that he was losing the struggle.

The knight was trying to use his sword against the kretch, but he was too close to it and his blows were ineffectual against the creature's armoured back. Sir Gilbert was no longer a young man. His stamina would be failing. Nor would the spikes on his armour be as effective against this beast as they had been against the worme. And now, to my dismay, I saw the jaws of the kretch close about the knight's head and bite down hard, and I heard the armour crumple. Its jaws were powerful and able to exert great leverage; now its teeth were penetrating his skull. I heard groans of dismay from the knight's men and knew that Will would be watching his father's plight in anguish.

It was then that what I had both feared and expected happened. The witches, led by Bowker, surged out of the mist and, whooping and shrieking, ran towards the river bank, where the combatants still struggled. Most carried knives. As before, the three at the front were armed with blades lashed to the end of long poles so that they could cut stab and cut from a distance. The knight was facing the same fate that had befallen the lamia; the difference here was that a determined and sizeable force was able to intervene. All was not lost.

A guard called down a warning to those below, and I heard the rumble of the gate as it was opened.

'Stay close to me and don't attempt anything reckless!' I warned Thorne.

By the time we reached the gate it was open and the knight's men were already charging towards the river. Will was standing by the gate with two other men, gazing forlornly out towards the battle. As the only heir to the castle and lands, he would have been forbidden to join the fight.

We closed with them quickly, but I gestured to Thorne that we should hang back. Once the two groups came together we would be able to judge how and where to fight most effectively.

I looked ahead and saw that more witches had run out of the mist on our side of the river and were racing to intercept us, brandishing their weapons. Those on the far bank had engulfed the knight and the kretch – doubtless they were attempting to put an end to him as the beast held his head in its jaws, replicating what had been done to Wynde. Twice I had been powerless to prevent a death, but there might still be time to help Sir Gilbert. They would have to remove his armour to kill him. That would take time, allowing us to rescue him.

The knight's men came to a sudden halt. For a moment I thought they were about to turn and flee: the approaching hordes were a fearsome sight and outnumbered us many times over. But ours was truly a well-disciplined force and I heard a voice call out an order:

'Fire!'

The eight archers bent their bows and released their arrows, which sped unerringly towards their targets. Each arrow struck a witch. I saw at least three fall and another two stagger and spin. And already the archers had nocked fresh arrows from the quivers on their shoulders and were bending their bows again.

The order to fire came again, and with a *whoosh* another fusillade of arrows hit our enemies to even more deadly effect. They were almost upon us now, less than thirty yards away, but a third volley of arrows broke up their attack and the witches scattered.

However, they did not flee but began to encircle us, thinning out so as to present a more difficult target. The opening volleys had been fired simultaneously, but now the order was changed to:

'Fire at will!'

At this, each archer began to choose his own target – a less effective tactic because the witches were already using dark magic against us. They were chanting spells in the Old Tongue, and foremost amongst these was *Dread*. Its power was wasted on me and Thorne, for we had defences against such things, but to the archers and men-at-arms their enemies would now appear in hideous shapes, their faces twisting into daemonic caricatures, their mud-caked hair resembling writhing nests of poisonous snakes.

The spell was already working only too well: I saw the eyes of the nearest bowmen widen with fear and his bow tremble violently so that he released his arrow harmlessly into the ground. I had to act quickly or all would be lost. Now I must use all my strength and carry the fight to the enemy. The kretch and the mage must die!

CHAPTER
~16~
MUST WE RUN FOR EVER?

With a sharp blade in her hand,
a witch assassin dies fighting her enemies.
Why should it be any different for me?

Fingering my bone necklace, I used the spell which in the Latin tongue is called Imperium, but is known as Sway by the Mouldheel clan, who always like to do things differently. It is partly an exertion of the will, and it is important to pitch the command with a certain inflection of the voice. But if it is done properly, others will obey instantly.

There was fear and chaos all around me, and that helped. My voice cut through the uncertainty and I directed it at those nearest to me: three archers, two soldiers, and Thorne.

'*Follow me!*' I commanded, pitching my voice perfectly.

They turned as one and locked eyes with me. Only Thorne showed resistance, but she would obey me without the magic. The others were alert, responsive and utterly compliant.

Then I began to run towards the river, where the knight still struggled with the kretch on the far bank. The others followed close on my heels, but as I reached the first of the witches who encircled us, Thorne moved up to my right side. We fought together as one entity with a single purpose; four legs and four arms directed by a single mind. A blade was in my left hand and I swung it in a short lethal arc – and the nearest of my enemies perished. Out of the corner of my eye I saw Thorne despatch another of the witches.

We were a lethal force, and broke through the thin circle with ease. But when we crossed the ford, there were at least nine witches clustered about the place of combat, stabbing downwards at the knight. Lisa Dugdale was leaning on her pole, attempting to push the blade into the join between helmet and neck, always a weakness in such armour. But there was mail beneath and Sir Gilbert was doubly protected. However, the greatest threat to his life came from the kretch, which still had his head in its jaws; the metal of his helmet had crumpled inwards. Sir Gilbert was groaning with pain and still struggling to be free. His sword had fallen from his grasp but he was punching the head of the kretch repeatedly with his mailed fist.

I knew we had to act quickly because the witches behind us would regroup and we'd be cut off from the castle.

'*Use your bows!*' I commanded, and the three archers obeyed instantly, firing three arrows into the throng. One embedded itself in the nearest witch, hurling her backwards into the mud. After a second volley the kretch shook the body of the knight like a dog with a rat, before releasing its prey and bounding directly towards us. I met its eyes and saw that I was still the primary target.

I selected a throwing knife and hurled it straight at the beast; it embedded itself up to the hilt in the creature's right eye. Two arrows also found their target. One skidded harmlessly off its shoulder but the second went straight into its open mouth and pierced its throat. It was Thorne who put things beyond doubt. She threw her blade with great accuracy to take the creature in the left eye. Now it was blind.

It swerved away from us and bounded towards the trees, yelping like a whipped dog. Seconds later we reached Sir Gilbert, and the two soldiers lifted him out of the mud and began to carry him. There was no time to check on his condition but it didn't look good. Blood was leaking out of the crumpled helmet. We headed back across the river and joined up with those of our party who'd survived the battle. The sergeant gave an order and the men-at-arms formed a small tight defensive square about the archers and the soldiers carrying the wounded knight. But Thorne and I fought outside that square as we made a slow retreat back towards the castle gate.

Of the mage there was no sign, and this, added to the flight of the kretch, seemed to have disheartened our foes. Although they still outnumbered us many times over, few engaged us directly, and those who did died either at my hands or at Thorne's, while those who followed sullenly at a distance were picked off by the four archers who had survived the battle.

At last we made it into the castle; the portcullis was closed behind us and the drawbridge lowered. We had lost perhaps a third of our force, and of the survivors many had suffered wounds. Nevertheless our first priority was the welfare of Sir Gilbert, who was carried into the great hall and carefully laid upon a table, where his attendants began to remove his spiked armour. Will watched in anguish as his father moaned in pain; blood continued to leak copiously from the battered helmet. His arm was badly mangled too, and removing the chain-mail sleeve proved too difficult.

Leaving him dressed in his mail undergarment, they

next tried to remove his helmet, but he cried out in agony. I held up my hand to warn them to stop and pushed my way through to inspect him more closely. Then I shook my head.

'The helmet cannot be removed,' I told them. 'He is dying. All you can do is give him something for the pain.'

The jaws of the kretch had embedded the metal deep into the knight's skull. There would be pressure on the brain and it would swell and kill him. I estimated that he would be dead within a few hours at most.

'No! No! It cannot be so!' cried the son, starting to weep.

Thorne walked across and put her arm on his shoulder to comfort him, but he brushed her off angrily, glaring at her with hate-filled eyes. She stepped back, surprise and pain twisting her face.

I came forward, put my own arm on his shoulder and spoke to him in a kind voice. 'Your father was a brave man, Will, and his deeds will always be remembered. You must be strong. Eventually you will rule here.'

The boy pulled away from me and I could see anger surge into in his face again. 'I wish I had never brought you here!' he cried. 'You have caused my father's death!'

'I wish it had not happened,' I told him gently. 'But we cannot change the past.'

I turned and beckoned Thorne, and we left the hall to return to our rooms. In the corridor outside we met the priest, escorted by two soldiers. No doubt he had been summoned to pray for Sir Gilbert. He gave me a look of utter hatred as he passed, but I hardly glanced at him.

Back in our room, I explained the new situation to Thorne.

'We are in danger,' I warned her, 'and may soon have to fight for our lives against those who just moments ago were our allies.'

'Will seemed very angry. I thought we were friends,' she said bitterly. 'Do you think he'll turn against us?'

'It matters little what he would *like* to do, Thorne. He is a minor and thus too young to assume his

241

father's role yet. Don't you remember what Sir Gilbert said? On his death the priest will become the boy's guardian until he comes of age. That guardian will rule this castle. So it is time to make our escape lest this refuge becomes a prison that we leave only by dying.

'And there is another reason to leave now,' I continued. 'The kretch has been blinded. I believe that it will heal itself, but that will take time. So we should go now and put some distance between us.'

'But where can we go?' asked Thorne; she seemed close to despair. 'Must we run for ever? Will was the first boy I've ever liked. It seems hard to part in anger. Perhaps I should try to speak to him when he's calmed down a little.'

'You would be wasting your time, Thorne. It is not safe for either of us to remain here a moment longer. And once safely beyond this castle, we should split up,' I suggested. 'Our enemies are too numerous and they will never give up. Eventually they will catch me and kill me. But why should you die too? The clan will need a good assassin to replace me. You are the one, child.'

Thorne shook her head. 'No, I won't leave you. If you die I'll become the custodian of the head. Isn't that what you hoped?'

I nodded, realizing that she had made up her mind. I prepared to retrieve the leather sack but immediately I sensed danger. The warning came a moment too late. The door opened and four archers, bows at the ready, stepped inside. Behind them were another four men-at-arms and the priest, Father Hewitt.

'Lay down your weapons or die here!' he commanded.

He was a big man with broad shoulders and a florid complexion. Physically, he looked more like a burly farmer than a priest, but the black soutane he wore was new, with gleaming silver buttons down the front, and his shoes were cut from the finest leather.

Suddenly there were flickers of light in the corners of my eyes, the warning that the weakness was about to overcome me again. I had to get us out of the castle quickly.

'Is this the way to speak to allies who fought on your side so recently?' I demanded.

'Sir Gilbert has just died and I rule here now. No alliance can be made with witches. *Thou shalt not suffer a witch to live!*' he cried.

'So if we lay down our arms we die later? What sort of choice is that? I would rather die here, and I tell you this – not all of you will survive. I am Grimalkin, and I have already chosen those whom I will kill!'

'Surrender to us now,' said the priest, his voice suddenly softer and more reasonable, 'and you will receive a fair trial from the Holy Church.'

The flashing lights within my eyes were increasing in intensity. I had to act now if we were to escape.

'I have heard of such "fair trials",' I scoffed. 'What will you do? Crush our bodies with stones or drown us in the nearest deep pond? This is my answer!'

With that, I drew two blades and pointed them

towards the priest. But he smiled grimly and looked confident.

He said just one word:

'Fire!'

The four bowmen aimed at us and released their arrows.

CHAPTER 17
IT BRINGS GREAT DISHONOUR

My speed in combat is not dark magic;
it is the magic of my being,
the magic of who I am.
I am Grimalkin!

A witch assassin needs to be fast. I have that speed.
But will it be enough against master archers at
such close quarters? And what of Thorne, who is some
years short of reaching her full strength?

All these futile thoughts race through my head
while my limbs act instinctively.

I have trained my body so that it is a weapon:
every sinew, muscle and bone is coordinated; in such

a situation it does not need the brain to command it.

Thought is too slow.

I am diving forward, going into a roll. I stop my heart. I lift the blade in my left hand and deflect an arrow with it. Time seems to be passing very slowly. I think of Tom Ward, who has the power to slow time, and I laugh! A witch assassin can do it too – but in a different way. An assassin moves so quickly that it is the movements of others that appear to have slowed down.

It is not dark magic. It is the magic of my being; the magic of who I am; the magic of how hard I have trained. I am Grimalkin!

I exist in the 'now' and I deal out death.

I deflect another arrow and glance to my right. Thorne's actions mirror my own. We divide, converge and divide again, like water flowing over sharp rocks. I have trained her well and could not wish for a better student. When I die, she will replace me. No other Malkin will be able to stand against her in combat.

Now I am amongst my enemies and I begin to cut into them. An archer screams and dies. I must forget that I fought alongside these men so recently. We are in close now and they cannot use their bows. The situation has changed. It is their lives or ours. They know it too. Such is combat. We must kill or be killed. So I kill. I kill again and again, and the screams of the dying seem very far away.

I allow my heart to beat once; blood surges through my arteries.

I whirl and cut and spin and cut again. Enemy blood sprays everywhere; within seconds I will reach the priest. Once beyond his corpse, we will head for the gate. It can be done. We can win. We can escape.

But then, too soon, the breath catches in my throat and there is a sudden pain in my chest. Weakness quickly brings me to my knees. It is the poison of the kretch. I fight against it but all goes dark.

Is this death?

My last thought is of Thorne. She is so young, and now she will die too. I feel a moment of regret at bringing her into danger. Then there is darkness and I forget everything.

* * *

But I did not die then. I awoke with a taste of blood in my mouth, bound securely in a dark place.

Iron manacles clamped my hands and feet together; the metal was painful and I could feel it burning my skin. I was lying on my back against a damp wall. I rolled to my left, but half a turn brought me to a halt. There was another chain stretching from my feet to an iron ring in the stone floor.

I managed to sit up and rest my back against the wall. It was very dark, but with my witchy eyes I could see even into the gloomiest corners of that dungeon. It stank of death. Over the years a dozen or more had died here. Sir Gilbert had seemed benign, but clearly he had imprisoned people, some of whom had ended their days in this underground prison. What were their crimes? I wondered.

It mattered little. *My* crime was to be a witch. In the hands of the priest I could expect nothing but pain and death. The scryer had once predicted my death, but it had been in combat with a knife in my hand, not chained up helplessly. But scryers are not always completely accurate – there is always room for error.

I consoled myself with the thought that at least they would not find the Fiend's head. I had hidden it too well. Only very powerful practitioners of dark magic could discover its whereabouts, and they would have to get into this castle first. As the knight had told me, these walls could withstand weeks of siege. Every day that the head was kept out of their hands meant more time for Tom Ward to find a way to finish the Fiend for ever.

The weakness seemed to have passed but it mattered little now. Bound in iron chains, I had little chance of escaping. I still wore my leather straps but their sheaths were empty; my weapons were gone. However, I still had one weapon left – and the last of my magic. These were being saved as a final resort. The time to use them must be chosen with extreme care. After that it would be hopeless.

It was then that I heard the first scream. It was thin and high and lingered on the air: a female cry – the cry of someone suffering unendurable pain.

It came again, and it made the hairs on the back of my neck rise up in dread. Someone was being tortured.

Was it Thorne?

A second later my heart sank as I heard confirmation that it was.

'Please! Please!' she begged. 'Don't do that – anything but that!'

Thorne was brave and fearless. What kind of torture could make her beg like that, her voice so shrill and tremulous?

I could not stand by and hear her suffer so. But first I had to see exactly what the situation was, and I had the means to accomplish that without using too much of my remaining store of power. I would use shamanistic magic, and project my soul from my body once more.

I chanted the necessary words, getting the cadence exactly right, and concentrated on exerting my will. For a second all became dark, and then I was floating above my chained body again, in a world within which everything was a shade of green. I looked down on myself, at the closed eyes and deep, steady breathing, then drifted towards the dungeon door; my spirit passed right through it.

I emerged in the passage beyond, and it was easy to find the room where Thorne was being tortured. It was the next cell to the left. The door was wide open, and a guard, his body glowing green with life-force, was standing outside with his back against the wall. Once inside, I took in the situation with one glance.

Thorne lay on her back, tied to a metal table with thick ropes. There was blood on her bare shoulders and arms. A burly man was standing over her, stripped to the waist, his chest hairy and his skin gleaming with sweat. In his right hand he held a bodkin – he had been stabbing the long thin sharp point repeatedly into Thorne's body. They were trying to find the place where she had supposedly been touched by the Fiend; the place where she could feel no pain; the place that proved she was a witch.

All this was completely unnecessary: we were

clearly witches; we did not deny it. But the priest hovered close, wearing a smile on his thin lips. He was enjoying this.

And then I understood what it was that had caused Thorne to cry out and beg like that. It had little to do with the work of the bodkin on her body; little to do with the extreme pain that she must be suffering. No – what had caused her so much terror was the tool the priest was holding.

It was a pair of scissors that belonged to me; those with which I snipped away the thumb-bones of my dead enemies. The remainder of my weapons were aligned in a neat row on a small wooden table in the far corner of the room. But the priest must have known something of witch lore because he had selected the scissors.

Boiled up in a pot, accompanied by the correct rituals, thumb-bones bring dark magical power to their possessor. But losing her thumb-bones is one of the worst things that a witch can suffer. It brings great dishonour: all that a witch has achieved in her lifetime instantly becomes null and void. And such a fate is all the more terrible for a witch assassin. Having been exalted, feared and respected by her clan, she immediately becomes nothing more than an object of laughter and ridicule.

Although it is possible for a living witch to survive if her thumb-bones are taken, most die of shock after such a procedure. But even if they are taken after death, there may be consequences. It is believed that a dead witch thus maimed cannot be reborn; she cannot return to walk the earth once more. She must remain in the dark for ever.

No wonder Thorne had cried out in anguish at such a threat. For her the worst thing would be the shame and loss of respect. Not only had she hoped to become the greatest Malkin assassin of all time; she wanted that reputation to endure after her death. With two snips of those scissors the priest threatened to take that away from her.

I quickly took in the situation, noting the two other guards standing against the far wall. So there were four men to deal with in the room and one outside in the passage.

I retreated fast, jerking my spirit back into my body as quickly as I could. I opened my eyes and began to use the last of my magical resources, twisting my neck and projecting my tongue out as far as I was able. I curled it around the necklace and manipulated the final potent thumb-bone into my mouth. Next I sucked it, slowly drawing into my body the last of its stored power. That done, I released it and concentrated hard, focusing on the solitary guard outside the cell door.

My final shred of magic was certainly not strong enough to compel him to enter my cell and free me from my chains. But I could bring him to me in another way – by putting an element of doubt in his head; his duty would be to guard the passage, barring entry to the torture cell, but at the same time ensuring that I was safely confined. I used a simple spell that filled his mind with anxiety about me.

Seconds later he inserted a key into the lock, turned

it, opened the door, and came into my cell. He took two steps forward and stared at me intently. I held my breath. What I was about to attempt was difficult and I would only get one chance.

The wisdom tooth at the back of my lower left jaw is hollow. I'd drilled the deep thin hole myself with a tool I forged specially for the purpose. That tooth contains a fine needle coated with a poison that eats away at a person's will, making them malleable enough to obey another's commands. It is a poison to which I have built up an immunity over many years by taking very small doses and increasing them steadily; thus I can store the poisoned needle in my mouth without suffering any adverse effects.

I flicked aside the false top of the tooth with the tip of my tongue and sucked the needle out of the cavity. A second later it was positioned between my lips. I had practised this manoeuvre many times, but the needle was tiny and the guard still some distance away from me: success was far from certain.

At the last moment he started to turn away. Some

instinct of self-preservation must have made him aware of the danger. But he was too late. I spat the needle towards him with great force and it embedded itself in the side of his neck, just below his right ear. He staggered and almost fell, and a look of bewilderment settled across his face.

'Look at me!' I urged. 'Listen to all I say and obey every word without question!'

The guard stared at me. The poison had already taken effect. He was breathing noisily with his mouth open, and saliva was dribbling from his lower lip and dripping from his chin.

'Release me from my chains!' I commanded.

He came forward and did as I asked, but the poison made his movements slow, and he fumbled with the key. At any moment the priest might take Thorne's thumb-bones, but I had to stay calm and patient and wait to be released.

At last I was free. I took the guard's weapons – two daggers and a heavy club. I could have killed him then, but there was no need. Instead I told him to lie down and fall into a deep sleep. He was snoring before I left the cell.

Hoping against hope that I would not hear Thorne scream, I tiptoed into the passage. The moment I showed myself in the doorway to the cell, I attacked. The priest was gripping Thorne's left hand, the blades of the scissors wide open, as he prepared to snip away the first of her thumb-bones.

Faster than thought, I threw the blade in my left hand. My own weapons, particularly my throwing blades, are perfectly suited to their purpose – finely balanced and calibrated. I also practise with them constantly. This was an unfamiliar weapon and one designed for hand-to-hand combat – not throwing. So I took no chances.

Normally I would have gone for the throat or the eye; either shot would have slain the priest almost immediately. This time I buried my blade deep into his shoulder; it was an easy target and it caused him to drop the scissors. Besides, I had other plans for him; I could always kill him later if it proved necessary.

With the other blade and the club I attacked the two guards. I did not think; my body simply acted, guided by my long years of training, while my mind vibrated with the ecstasy of combat. Such was my speed that the first died before he could cry out; the second probably survived but the blow to his temple laid him out cold. The whole thing had lasted barely two seconds. Beyond was the burly torturer, still gripping the bodkin he had used on Thorne. He stabbed it towards me, but I dashed it aside with the club and killed him by driving my dagger up under his ribs and into his heart.

The priest was on his knees now, whimpering with pain. I threw the club aside, and when I tugged the blade from his flesh, he screamed; I used the knife to cut the ropes that bound Thorne to the table. The priest's cry did not alarm me; it was shrill and high and could well have been the cry of a girl being tortured. It would not bring others to investigate.

We had to get out of the castle, and I intended to use the priest as our hostage. The main barriers to our escape were the remaining archers. They could kill us from a distance.

'You're safe,' I told Thorne, helping her from the table. 'I know you are hurt and have endured an experience that might have broken the mind of a strong witch. But it is important that you gather yourself and prepare for danger. Are you ready – or do you need a few more moments to compose yourself?'

'I'm ready now,' Thorne answered, giving me a brave smile, her voice little more than a croak. I was proud of her at that moment; she had become more than I ever hoped for.

'Then first we have to retrieve the head of the Fiend.'

After returning my blades and scissors to their sheaths, I tore a strip from the hem of the priest's cassock and used that to gag him. As I dragged him along, he made no attempt to resist; he looked terrified. We reached our chamber without incident, and soon the leather sack was safely on my shoulder once more.

Pushing the priest ahead of us, we reached the castle yard. It was dark outside, with heavy cloud, and three hours at least till dawn. That would make it more difficult for the archers.

There was a soldier on guard, standing with his back to the portcullis. He held a flickering torch aloft as we approached. It illuminated the figure of the priest first, and I saw the man's expression of deference and obedience change to incredulity and fear as he saw the priest's terrified face and the blood-soaked arm of his cassock.

I held a blade to the priest's throat. 'We are leaving. Prepare our way or he dies!'

With shaking hands the soldier began to raise the portcullis by turning the capstan. The clanks and rattles of the chains sounded very loud in the darkness. That would attract attention. Others would wonder why someone should be leaving or entering the castle at such an hour.

A voice called down from the battlements: 'Who goes there? Show yourselves!'

We stepped closer to the wall and pressed ourselves into the shadows. The portcullis was rising very slowly. At last it was high enough for us to duck underneath.

'That's enough. Now get that door open! Do it quickly!' I said, gripping the priest by the hair and pressing the blade against his throat.

The frightened soldier hastened to obey, and unlocked the door quickly, pulling it inwards until it was wide open, revealing the outer portcullis and the drawbridge beyond. He didn't wait to be told to work the second capstan, and the portcullis was raised faster this time.

But now I could hear distant shouts of command and footsteps running towards us across the darkness of the yard. We did not enter the gateway, fearing that we might be targeted from the side, as we had been when we'd entered this place. We prepared to meet their attack and I brought them into focus with my keen eyes. They were not archers; just three men armed with pikes.

'They are yours, Thorne!' I hissed. I knew that after suffereing the pain of the torture it would be good for her to get back into action as soon as possible.

'All three?'

'Yes, but make it quick!'

Thorne whirled forward to meet them just as I had taught her. She was fast, and her combat skills were honed almost to perfection. Some had been acquired by long hours of practice, but there were some things that cannot be taught; Thorne had the art born in her, and with consummate grace she avoided the hastily jabbed pikes of the soldiers, and her blades flashed, dealing out death to all three in a matter of seconds.

I could see that within two years Thorne would be my equal.

And after that?

Eventually she would be capable of defeating me just as I had defeated Kernolde. The thought brought me happiness, not fear. I would not wish to live once my powers began to decline. It was good to know that I had a worthy successor.

The soldier was lowering the drawbridge now, but other footsteps were racing towards us through the darkness. This time I did not order Thorne to attack. One of those approaching was smaller than the rest. It was Will, the son of the dead knight.

The group halted about twenty paces from us – five men; the two flanking the boy were the last of the master bowmen.

'Release Father Hewitt!' cried the boy. 'It's a sin to harm a priest!'

'Tell your men to put down their weapons and I will allow him to live,' I said softly. 'If you refuse, then I will kill this poor excuse for a priest and you will be responsible for his death.'

'You caused my father's death!' Will screamed hysterically. 'Now you will die too!'

He put his hands on the shoulders of the archers who flanked him. 'Aim low!' he cried. 'They will try to dive beneath your arrows!'

The archers raised their bows and fired.

CHAPTER
18
YOU'RE JUST A GIRL

I chose to bear the Fiend's child
so as to be free of him for ever;
and, once I'd decided to pursue that course,
nothing could ever have stopped me.
My intention is to destroy him.
Nothing will stop me now!

Faster than the flight of the arrow, I yanked the priest
in front of me, pushing him to his knees as a shield.
They fired low as commanded, and an arrow embedded
itself in his chest. He gave a groan of pain and fell, stone
dead, to the ground. I glanced to my left and saw that
Thorne had deflected the other arrow with her blade.

Before the archers could pull further arrows from their quivers our throwing blades pierced the left eye-socket of each and the bows slipped from their dead fingers as they crumpled at the feet of the boy.

He took a step backwards, terror animating his features. But what would it profit us to slay him? I asked myself. He was just a child whose world had been turned upside down. I could read a whole range of emotions on Thorne's face. There was anger and outrage at Will, who had tried to kill us, but also sadness and regret. I knew that she felt betrayed.

'The priest is dead, Will,' I told him with a grim smile. 'Your guardian has been retired from his duties. You are in charge here now. Rule wisely and rule well!'

Will looked at Thorne and tried to speak, but the drawbridge was almost down now and we couldn't wait. With Thorne at my heels, I ran up its slippery wooden incline and leaped the narrowing gap to land on the soft earth at the far edge of the moat. Arrows whistled towards us from the battlements but we were running fast, weaving from side to side, and these were not masters of their craft. In a few seconds we were lost in the safety of the darkness.

The real danger now lay somewhere ahead. Had the kretch regenerated itself yet? Would the mage and the witches know that we had left the castle?

The answer to my first question was uncertain, but it was likely that spies would be watching. They would have heard the shouts and seen the drawbridge being lowered. Even now they would be alerting their sister witches.

So we ran hard in a direction that was roughly east, towards the rising sun. I was thinking desperately: *Where could we go? What refuge remained?*

My mind twisted first one way then another, seeking what was not there to be found. It was true that there was one place we might use to our advantage, although we might encounter more enemies than friends there. I changed direction and picked up my pace.

'Witch Dell lies directly ahead!' Thorne said, running alongside me.

'Yes, that's where we are heading, child. It may prove a good place to stand and fight!'

Before long Pendle Hill dominated the skyline. It was shaped like a huge whale – the great sea mammal that I had glimpsed on one of my journeys across the great northern sea that lay beyond the borders of the County.

We rested for a while in a wood, confident that we had put a good distance between us and our pursuers. We would not approach Witch Dell until nightfall.

I turned to Thorne. 'How do you feel, child?' I asked. I wondered whether her experiences in the dungeon might affect her ability to fight.

'Feel?' she snapped. 'Feel about what – the boy?'

'Yes, the boy – and also the physical hurt that you received.'

'The boy is nothing to me now. Are all men fools like that?'

'Not all men are fools, but there are plenty of dolts to spare for women who want them. But do not think too badly of Will. He lost his father – and, by making a bargain with us, set up the chain of events that led to his father's death. But forget him now. He is in the past and could never have been part of your life anyway. You are a witch and will soon become a fully-fledged assassin. He will become a knight. You come from different worlds.'

'Yes, I will try to forget him. I will push him from my mind.'

Thorne fell silent, so after a while I spoke again. 'What about the torture?' I asked.

'The pain of being stabbed with the bodkin was terrible at first,' Thorne answered, 'but after a while I grew less sensitive and coped better. The priest realized that, so he threatened to take my thumb-bones. He was enjoying my fear and really meant to cut them from me while I still lived. I could read it in his eyes. It was unbearable. Never have I felt such terror and despair. All that I have been and could have become would have been taken from me. I would have been nothing – a shameful thing to be ridiculed for ever.'

'Well, it did not happen, child. You were brave and

bore the pain well. The priest is dead and you live to fight another day. We *will* destroy our enemies and prevail.'

'Will we be safe in the dell?' Thorne asked. 'Will we find allies there?'

'Nowhere on this earth is safe for us now, child. But it depends whom we encounter first. Some of the dead may be well-disposed towards us; most will just want our blood. But they will protect their territory. If we can get into the heart of the dell, they will defend it against the larger threat of those who pursue us.'

'Witch Dell is the place where you fought Kernolde and became the witch assassin, isn't it?' Thorne asked.

'It is indeed, child. Years have passed but it seems like only yesterday.'

'Tell me about it,' Thorne asked.

'You know the story well. You've heard it from my own lips more than once.'

I listened to the wind sighing through the trees and checked our surroundings for danger. All was clear. Our enemies were still some distance away.

'Then please tell it one more time. Stories change a little with each telling. A good teller of tales remembers new things and forgets what is least important.'

I sighed, but then began my tale. Why not? It would distract us both for a while from the danger that lay ahead and behind.

'The challenge always took place north of the three villages of the Malkins, Deanes and Mouldheels; the spot was usually selected by the then assassin.

'Kernolde chose as her killing ground Witch Dell, where she routinely used these dead things as her allies, the only witch who has ever done so success-fully. More than one challenger was drained of blood by the dead before Kernolde took her thumb-bones as proof of victory.'

'Wasn't that cheating – to use dead witches to aid her?' Thorne asked.

'Some might think so, but she had been the Malkin assassin for many years. She was feared. Who would dare to question what she did?'

'I've heard that some of the dead witches are really

strong and can roam for miles seeking their prey. How many are there at present like that?' Thorne asked.

'There were five until autumn, but as you know even dead witches do not survive for ever. Gradually they weaken, and parts of their bodies begin to decay and fall off. I learned from Agnes that the winter took its toll; now there are only three really strong ones.'

'Who will they side with – you or our enemies?'

'That is uncertain, child. But if at least two fight alongside us, the balance of power will be in our favour.'

Thorne nodded, deep in thought. 'Tell me more about Kernolde,' she demanded.

'Kernolde often proved victorious without her dead allies. She was skilled with blades, ropes, traps and pits full of spikes, but her speciality was strangulation. Once they were defeated she invariably strangled her opponents. She enjoyed inflicting that slow death upon those she had overcome.

'I knew this long before my challenge began: I'd thought long and hard about it and had visited the dell many times during the previous months. I had usually gone there in daylight, when the dead witches were dormant and Kernolde was out hunting prey. I had sniffed out every inch of the wood; knew every tree, every blade of grass; the whereabouts of every pit and trap. And there were lots of those. Some who fought Kernolde died even before they reached her.

'So I was ready: I stood outside the dell in the shadow of the trees just before midnight, the appointed time for combat to begin. High to my left was the large mass of Pendle Hill, its eastern slopes bathed in the light of the full moon, which had risen high to the south. Within moments a beacon flared at the summit, sparks shooting upwards into the air to signal the beginning of my challenge.

'Immediately I did what no other challenger had done before. Most crept into the dell, nervous and fearful, in dread of what they faced. Some were braver but still entered cautiously. I was different. I announced my presence in a loud clear voice.'

'Let me say it for you, Grimalkin. Please!' Thorne interrupted.

I nodded, and Thorne got to her feet, put on a very serious face and called out the words that I had used all those long years ago:

'"I'm here, Kernolde! My name is Grimalkin and I am your death!"' she shouted at the top of her voice. '"I'm coming for *you*, Kernolde! I'm coming for *you*! And nothing living or dead can stop me!"'

She sat down and we both laughed for a while. 'Did you mean it?' Thorne asked. 'Did you really believe your own words?'

'To a certain extent I believed. It was not just bravado, although that played no small part. My behaviour was a product of much thought and calculation. I knew that my shouts would bring the dead witches towards me, and that's what I wanted. Now I would know where they were. It is always important to spy out the location of any danger that we face.

'Most dead witches are slow, and I knew that I could outpace them. It was the powerful ones I had to beware of. One of them was named Gertrude the Grim because of her intimidating and repulsive appearance, and she was both strong and quick for one who had been dead for more than a century. She roamed far and wide beyond the dell, hunting for blood. But tonight she would be waiting within it, for she was Kernolde's closest accomplice, well-rewarded in blood for aiding each victory.

'I waited for fifteen minutes or so, long enough to let the slowest witch get near to me. I'd already sniffed out Gertrude, the old one. She'd been close to the edge of the dell for some time but had chosen not to venture out into the open; she had moved in amongst the trees so that her slower sisters could threaten me first. I could hear the rustling of leaves and the occasional faint crack of a twig as they shuffled forward. They were slow, but never underestimate a dead witch. They have great strength, and once they have hold of your flesh they cannot easily be prised free. Soon they begin to suck your blood, until you weaken and can fight no more. Some would be in the ground, hiding within the dead leaves and mud, ready to reach out and grasp at my ankles as I sped by.

'I sprinted into the trees. I had already sniffed out Kernolde and she was exactly where I expected, waiting beneath the branches of the oldest oak in the dell. This was her tree; the one in which she stored her magic; her place of power.'

I enjoyed telling the tale to Thorne and thus reliving my fight to become the witch assassin. I have won many battles since, but that first victory brought me the greatest enjoyment because it was where Grimalkin truly began.

'A hand reached up towards me from the leaves. Without breaking stride, I slipped a dagger from the scabbard on my left thigh and pinned the dead witch to the thick gnarled root of a tree. And here is some good advice for you, Thorne. Never pin a witch through the palm of her hand – she can simply tear herself free. Always thrust your blade into the wrist rather than the palm. And that is what I did.

'Another witch shuffled towards me from the right, her hideous face lit by a shaft of moonlight. Rivulets of saliva dribbled down her chin and dripped onto her tattered gown, which was covered in dark stains. She jabbered curses at me, eager for my blood. Instead she got my blade, which I plucked from my right shoulder sheath, hurling it towards her. The point took her in the throat, throwing her backwards. I ran on even faster.

'Four more times my blades speared dead flesh, and by now the other witches were left behind; the slow and those I'd maimed. But Kernolde and the powerful old one waited somewhere ahead. I wore eight sheaths that day; each contained a blade. Now only two remained.

I leaped a hidden pit; then a second. Although they were covered with leaves and mud, I knew they were there. At last Grim Gertrude barred my path. I came to a halt and awaited her attack. Let her come to me! Her tangled hair fell down to her knees. She was grim indeed, and well-named! A worm wriggled and dropped from her left nostril. Maggots and beetles scuttled through the slimy curtain that obscured all of her face save one malevolent eye; that and an elongated black tooth that jutted upwards over her top lip almost as far as her left nostril.

'She ran towards me, kicking up leaves, her hands extended to claw at my face or squeeze my throat. She was fast for a dead witch; very fast. But not fast enough. With my left hand, I drew the largest of my blades from its scabbard at my hip. As you know, this knife is not crafted for throwing; it is more akin to a short sword, with razor-sharp edges. I leaped forward to meet Grim Gertrude, and with one blow I cut her head clean from her shoulders.

'It bounced on a root and rolled away. I ran on, glancing back to see her searching amongst the pile of rotting leaves where it had come to rest.'

'Is Gertrude still to be found in the dell?' Thorne asked.

'There are few sightings of her now,' I answered. 'She is failing, her mind decaying more quickly than her body. No doubt I hastened her demise. But back to my story . . . Once Gertrude was dealt with, I was ready to face Kernolde. She was waiting beneath her tree; ropes hung from the branches, ready to bind and hang my body. She was rubbing her back against the bark, drawing strength for the fight. But I was not afraid – to me she looked like an old she-bear ridding herself of fleas rather than the dreaded witch assassin feared by all. Running at full pelt straight for her, I drew the last of my throwing knives and hurled it at her throat. End over end it spun, my aim fast and true, but she knocked it to one side with a disdainful flick of her wrist. Undaunted, I increased my pace and prepared to use the long blade. But then the ground opened up beneath my feet, my heart lurched and I fell into a hidden pit.

'I remember my feeling of shock at that moment. I had been so confident, but as I fell I realized that I had underestimated my opponent. A speedy victory had been snatched away – however, I was resilient and still determined to survive and fight on.

'The moon was high, and as I fell I saw the sharp spikes waiting to impale me. I twisted desperately, trying to avoid them, but it was impossible. All I could do was contort myself so that my body suffered the least damage.

'The least, did I say? The spike hurt me enough; damaged me badly. It pierced my outer thigh and I bear the scar to this day. Down its length I slid, until I hit the ground hard and all the breath left my body, the long blade flying from my hand to lie out of reach. I lay there in agony, struggling to breathe and control the extreme pain in my leg. The spikes were sharp, thin and very long – more than six feet – so there was no way I could lift my leg and free it. I cursed my folly. I had thought myself safe, but Kernolde had dug another pit – probably the previous night. No doubt she'd been aware of my forays into the dell and had waited until the very last moment to add this extra trap.

'A witch assassin must constantly adapt and learn from her mistakes. Even as I lay there, facing imminent death, I recognized my stupidity. I had been too confident. If I survived, I swore to temper my attitude with a smidgeon of caution.

'Kernolde's broad moon-face appeared above me, and she looked down without uttering a word. I was fast and I excelled with blades. I was strong too, but not as strong as Kernolde. Not for nothing did some call her Kernolde the Strangler. As I've told you, once victorious, Kernolde usually hung her victims by their thumbs before slowly asphyxiating them. Not this time though. She had seen what I had achieved already and would take no chances. I would die here.

'She began to climb down into the pit, preparing to place her powerful hands about my throat and squeeze the breath and life from my body. I was calm and ready to die if need be – but I had already thought of something. I had a slim chance of survival.

'As Kernolde reached the bottom of the pit and began to weave her way towards me through the spikes, flexing her big muscular hands, I prepared myself to cope with pain – not the pain that she would inflict upon me; that which I chose myself. My hands and arms and shoulders were very strong. The spikes were thin but sturdy; flexible, not brittle. But I had to try. Seizing the one that pierced my leg, I began to bend it. Back and forth, back and forth, I flexed and twisted the spike, each movement sending pain shooting down my leg and up into my body. But I gritted my teeth and worked the spike ever harder, until finally it yielded and broke, coming away in my hands.

'Quickly, I lifted my leg clear of the stump and knelt to face Kernolde, my blood running down to soak the earthen floor of the killing pit. I held the spike like a spear and pointed it towards her. Before her hands could reach my throat I would pierce her heart.

'Seeing that I had freed myself and was prepared to fight on, Kernolde looked astonished, but she quickly recovered herself and attacked me in a new way. She had drawn much of her stored magic from the tree, and now she halted and concentrated, hurling shards of darkness towards me. She tried *Dread* first, and terror tried to claim me. My teeth began to chitter-chatter like those of the dead on the Halloween sabbath. Her magic was strong; but not strong enough. I braced myself and shrugged aside her spell. Soon its effects receded and it bothered me no more than the cold wind that blew down from the arctic ice when I slew the wolves and left their bodies bleeding into the snow.

'Next she used the unquiet dead, hurling towards me the spirits she had trapped in Limbo. They clung to my body, leaning hard on my arm to bring it down, and it took all my strength to keep hold of the spike.'

'Have you ever trapped spirits in Limbo?' Thorne asked.

'I have in the past – but not any longer. That is why I have not taught you that skill. As assassins, we are better than your common bone-witch. We use magic, yes, but our greatest strength lies in the combat skills that we acquire and in our strength of mind. It was the latter that enabled me to repulse Kernolde's spirits. They were strong and fortified by dark magic: one was a strangler that gripped my throat so hard that Kernolde herself might have been squeezing it. The worst of them was an abhuman spirit, the ghost of one born of the Fiend and a witch. He darkened my eyes and thrust his long cold fingers into my ears so that I thought my head would burst, but I fought back and cried out into the darkness and silence:

'"I'm still here, Kernolde! Still to be reckoned with. I am Grimalkin, your doom!"

'My eyes cleared, and the abhuman's fingers left my ears with a pop so that sound rushed back. The weight was gone from my arms, and I struggled to my feet, taking aim with the spike. Kernolde rushed at me then – that big ugly bear of a woman with her strangler's hands. But my aim was true. I thrust the spear right into her heart and she fell at my feet, her blood soaking into the earth to mix with mine. She was choking, trying to speak, so I bent and put my ear close to her lips.

'"You're just a girl," she croaked. "To be defeated by a girl after all this time . . . How can this be?"

'"Your time is over and mine is just beginning," I told her. "This girl took your life and now she will take your bones."

'I watched her die; then, after taking her thumb-bones, which were very powerful and supplied me with magic for many months, I lifted her body out of the pit using her own ropes. Finally I hung her by her feet so that at dawn the birds could peck her clean. That done, I passed through the dell without incident, the dead witches keeping their distance. Grim Gertrude was on her hands and knees, still rooting through the sodden leaves, trying to find her head. Without eyes it would prove difficult and would keep her occupied for a long time.

'When I emerged from the trees, the clan was waiting to greet me. I held up Kernolde's thumb-bones and they bowed their heads in acknowledgement of what I'd done; even Katrise, the head of the coven of thirteen, made obeisance. When they looked up, I saw the new respect in their eyes; the fear too.

'With that victory, my quest to destroy my enemy, the Fiend, began. The spikes in the pit had given me an idea. What if I crafted a sharp spike of silver alloy and somehow impaled the Fiend on it?'

'Is that what you actually did to the Fiend before you cut off his head?' Thorne asked.

I nodded. 'Yes, child – with the help of Tom Ward and his master, John Gregory, I impaled the Fiend with silver spears and nailed his hands and feet to the rock. Then the Spook's apprentice cut the Fiend's head from his shoulders and I placed it in this leather sack. We filled the pit with earth, then sealed it with a large flat stone, finally placing a boulder on top of that. Until this head is returned to its body the Fiend is securely bound.'

'It will never be returned to its body,' Thorne said. 'Even if one of us dies, the other will continue to be its custodian. Then one day the Fiend will be destroyed for ever!'

There came a deep groan from the sack. The Fiend had been listening to our conversation and had not liked what he'd heard. In the long silence that followed, I could almost hear Thorne thinking. At last she spoke. It was a probing question.

'Have you ever taken the thumb-bones of your enemies while they were still alive?' she asked.

No doubt the threat to her own thumb-bones was

fresh in her mind, but before I could control myself I let out a hiss of anger.

'It's just that some say that is what you do to those you hate most,' Thorne continued quickly.

'My enemies must fear me,' I replied. 'With my scissors I snip the flesh of the dead; the clan enemies that I have slain in combat. Then I cut out their thumbbones, which I wear around my neck as a warning to others. What else would I do? Without ruthlessness and savagery I could not survive even a week of the life I lead.'

'But *the living*? Have you ever done it to the living?' Thorne persisted. She was brave to pursue the matter when I was clearly angry – courage was one of her best qualities. But it also displayed another side of her; a fault. She could be reckless. She did not know when to back off.

'I do not wish to speak of it,' I said quietly. 'The matter is closed.'

CHAPTER 19
WITCH DELL

I have looked into the darkness,
into the greatest darkness of all,
and now I fear nothing.

One hour after nightfall we approached the dell but halted beneath the wide branches of a solitary oak a hundred yards short of its nearest trees.

'Call her,' I whispered.

The night of the full moon had been and gone. Somewhere within those trees Agnes Sowerbutts would now have awoken to a new existence as a dead witch. In time, as her body slowly decayed, a witch sometimes became bitter and twisted, hating all those whom they had befriended and cared for in life. But those taken to the dell did not change their loves, hatreds and allegiances immediately. To a certain extent she would still be the same Agnes, and I hoped that we could rely on her to effect our safe entry to the dell – or at least to let us know the situation there.

Thorne gave a long mournful cry – something close to that made by a corpse-fowl but subtly modified into the signal that she always used when approaching Agnes's cottage. I had introduced Thorne to the old witch soon after I had begun her training and Agnes had taken the child under her wing, teaching her about potions, and occasionally, when I was away from Pendle, offering her a place to stay.

We waited in silence. There were faint rustles in the distant trees but nothing alive or dead ventured into the open. After about five minutes I instructed Thorne to try again. Once more we waited while the wind sighed through the branches of the oak. It was a night of sudden showers, and at that moment a particularly heavy one was falling; for a while all we could hear was rain drumming on the ground. The shower passed as quickly as it had started, and the moon came out briefly. It was then that I saw the dark shape crawling towards us across the clearing. Without doubt it was a dead witch. I could hear her sniffing and snuffling, her nose almost touching the wet grass, her gown a slithering shadow. Only when she lifted her face into the moonlight did I recognize her as Agnes. Death had already changed her for the worse.

She came in under cover of the branches, gasping and wheezing, and pulled herself up into a sitting position, resting her back against the tree trunk. For a while nobody spoke, and I listened to the drops of water dripping from leaf to leaf on their long slow journey to the ground.

I looked at Agnes with my keen eyes, and she was a sorry sight indeed. Some dead witches are strong and can run for miles, hunting human prey; others are weak, and theirs is a miserable existence crawling through the slime and leaf-mould, searching for small creatures such as rats and mice. If this was indeed Agnes's existence now, I pitied her. She had always been a proud woman; although at first glance her cottage had appeared cluttered, her bottles and jars were placed in perfect order upon her shelves and her house was immaculate – never even a speck of dust in sight. Very few witches cared about cleanliness; Agnes had been the exception. She had changed her clothes every day and her pointy shoes were so highly polished that you could see your refection in them.

Thorne looked shocked and momentarily covered her face with her hands. I too was dismayed to see the change that had befallen Agnes in so short a time. Her tattered dress was caked in dirt. No doubt she'd been crawling through brambles in search of prey. As for her once clean, shining hair, it was now greasy and infested with wriggling white maggots, while her gaunt face was smeared with mud and blood.

There was no point in trying to pretend that things were better than they appeared. Agnes had always been kind but plain-speaking, so I didn't mince my words, even though she was dead.

'It sorrows me to see you in this state, Agnes,' I told her kindly. 'Is there anything that we can do to help?'

'I never thought I would come to this,' she said, shaking her head so that maggots dropped from her hair into her lap. 'I was strong in life and hoped to be the same in death. But I thirst! I thirst so much and can never get enough blood. I am not strong enough to hunt large creatures or humans. Small rodents are all I can manage. Rabbits are too fast.'

'Don't the other dead help? Don't the strong help those weaker than themselves?' asked Thorne.

Agnes shook her head. 'Dead witches hunt alone and care for nought but themselves.'

'Then at least tonight your thirst will be quenched.' I said. I turned to Thorne: 'Bring Agnes something large.'

In an instant the girl had sped away.

'I still have the Fiend's head,' I told Agnes. 'It is in

all our interests that it remains detached from his body. Will you help? Our enemies are approaching, and we need to take refuge in the dell. We need some of our dead sisters to fight alongside us.'

'Others rule here,' Agnes croaked. 'I am feeble and my word counts for little within that dark place.'

'Are those within *for* the Fiend or *against* him?' I asked.

'Dead witches, be they strong or weak, care for nothing but blood. If they think at all, it is blood that fills their thoughts. I hope that I will never be like them. My memories of my life are precious and I want to hold onto them for as long as I can. But you needn't attempt to win them to your cause. They will kill anything living that enters the dell – you too if they can catch you.'

'How many of the strong ones are close at hand?' I said, listening to the rustles and scratching sounds from the dell, which told me that some of the weaker witches were close by.

'Only two. The third has been away for more

than two nights but could return at any time.'

'It is as I thought. So if we can get to the centre of the dell before our enemies arrive, the dead will effectively be our allies whether they wish it or not.'

I looked up and saw that Thorne was crossing the clearing towards us. Each hand held a large wriggling hare. She reached us and held one out to Agnes. The dead witch seized the frightened animal, then immediately sank her teeth into its neck and began to suck its blood. Within moments it had stopped twitching; it was drained and dead. Then she started on the second one.

'You're a good girl, Thorne!' Agnes cried when she'd finished. 'That's the sweetest blood I've sipped since coming to this miserable dell.'

'I wish I could do more for you,' Thorne said. 'You've always been good to me, Agnes, and it pains me to see you like this.'

Suddenly I sensed danger and sniffed the wind. Our enemies were close at hand.

'They're no more than ten minutes away,' I told

Thorne. 'It's a risk, but we need to take refuge in the dell now, before it's too late.' I turned to Agnes. 'Follow as best you can.'

I led Thorne to the edge of the dell. 'There are still pits and traps – those crafted by Kernolde many years ago. Some I will avoid; others I'll leap. We must move fast but follow close on my heels.'

So I sprinted into the dell, taking the same route that I had taken all those years earlier when I fought Kernolde. But this time no dead hands reached up to clutch my ankles now. Last time I had called out a challenge and drawn the witches towards me; this time we had the element of surprise, and the dead would be scattered amongst the trees. Only the two very strongest and fastest might be able to intercept us. And we were lucky, as the third had already left the dell to hunt. She might roam for miles and spend several nights away before returning. Or she could reappear at any moment.

I still had the exact location of each pit clear in my mind, and soon I was leaping over the first one. I never even glanced back to see if Thorne was safe. The girl was as sure-footed as I was and her reactions were just as quick.

Soon I sprang over a second, then a third, but at one point I dodged left to avoid a long thin pit that was impossible to jump: a tree trunk formed a barrier at its far edge. I remembered the way in which Kernolde had tricked and almost defeated me – by digging an extra pit that was unknown to me and filling it with sharp stakes to spear me. A sudden thought struck me.

What if she had dug other pits? What if there were ones that I was unaware of?

I calmed myself, picking up my pace through the dell. Such pits might or might not exist. But as long as I took the same route as last time, we would surely come to no harm.

Soon Kernolde's tree came into view; it was an ancient oak, the tree within which she had stored her magic. Despite the action of the elements during the intervening years, some of the ropes still hung down from the branches. From those she had once hung her defeated enemies.

I motioned to Thorne and we came to a halt. I pointed to the pit with my forefinger. It was still partially covered with branches and bracken, onto which many autumns had layered a bed of mouldering brown leaves. But at the edge I saw the large hole through which I had fallen, to be impaled below. We walked around the pit and turned, leaning our backs against the huge tree trunk as once Kernolde had done. It was strange to return to this place after all these years. My life had circled me back to the same spot, and I somehow sensed that I would soon face a similar crisis.

There was a rustling to my right. Something was approaching. No doubt it was one of the weaker dead witches – no real threat. After a few moments there were other louder sounds: the breaking of twigs underfoot, the heavy confident steps of someone who was not afraid to betray their presence.

A dead witch came into view. She was tall, but even if I had known her in life she would have been a stranger to me now. In place of her right eye was a black empty socket, and the flesh on that side of her face was missing, to reveal the skull and cheekbone. The remaining eye, however, glared at me with hatred. There was something very unusual about this dead witch too. Into the leather belt that held up her blood-splattered skirt was tucked a long blade with a curved handle shaped like a ram's horn, and she carried a long thin spear.

Dead witches don't usually arm themselves in this way. Their extreme strength, claws and teeth are sufficient weapons.

Suddenly I knew her, and everything was instantly clear. This was Needle, one of my predecessors, the witch assassin who had been defeated by Kernolde. Such a clan sister could have been an ally, but the hostile stare of her remaining eye said otherwise. It was filled with madness.

'You have crossed a line!' Needle hissed. '*I* rule here. This is the place of the dead, not the living. Do you come to challenge me, Grimalkin?'

'Why should the living challenge the dead?' I demanded. 'Your time is over. Kernolde defeated you and I defeated her. One day my time will also be over, and I will take my place here alongside you. We should be allies. There is a dangerous foe approaching.'

'Kernolde used trickery. She used the dead in her cause. Had she fought fairly, I would have defeated her, and in time you too would have died at my hands. So let us put that to the test now. Let us fight now – just the two of us!'

'First help me to defeat our common enemy,' I asked. 'What do you say?'

'Who is this enemy?'

'They are supporters of the Fiend. They want what I carry within this bag.'

I untied the sack, lifted out the head of the Fiend and showed it to Needle.

She smiled grotesquely and her white skull-bone gleamed in a shaft of moonlight. 'I have no love for the Fiend,' she said. 'But neither do I care for you! They call you the greatest of the Malkin assassins. It is a lie!'

I returned the Fiend's head to the sack and was just preparing to tie it shut when madness flickered in Needle's remaining eye and she ran at me, the spear pointing towards my heart.

I dropped the sack and the head, and prepared to defend myself. The most powerful of the dead witches were fast and very strong; much stronger than the living could hope to be. They could tear off my limbs with their bare hands. But this was worse: Needle was a trained witch assassin with a fearsome reputation. She would not be easy to overcome.

Thorne drew a blade and started to move towards my side, but I waved her back – my pride bade me deal with this dead assassin alone. At the last moment I twisted my body aside and the point of the spear missed me by inches. My blade was in my hand but I did not use it. Once I had cut the head from a dead witch in this very dell. To stop Needle I would have to do something similar – maybe even cut her into pieces. I decided to try to reason with her one more time. I still hoped that she might become our ally.

'Help me to defeat our enemies and *then* we will fight,' I offered.

'We fight now!' she cried. 'I will kill you then cut out your heart, sending you straight into the dark! Your thumb-bones too I will take. You will be without honour, obliterated from the history of Malkin assassins. You will be *nothing*!'

She ran at me, wielding the spear again. She was beyond reason, having nursed her grievance all through the long years she had spent with the dead. I had my back to the pit and knew exactly what to do. Once again I avoided the spear, and this time delivered a blow with my fist to the back of her head. She fell into the pit without uttering a single cry. But once impaled upon Kernolde's spikes she began to wail like a banshee.

'I was told that a dead witch doesn't feel pain,' Thorne said, looking down to where Needle was transfixed by the long thin spikes. Each was over six feet long and very thin. Four had pierced her body, and she had slid down them, right to the bottom of the pit. One had taken her in the left shoulder, another through the throat. One had speared her chest, the fourth her abdomen.

I noted the broken spike that I had snapped off to free myself and remembered my own pain.

'What you've heard is incorrect,' I told Thorne. 'She is in pain all right, but she is mainly screaming with frustration at failing to kill me. She knows that she lost and, what is worse, that I defeated her very easily. Her body may still be strong but her mind is rotting and she's fallen into madness. I overestimated her – she is a shadow of her former self.'

I almost pitied her, for she had fallen far from the heights she had once scaled as an assassin. I could only hope that I would never be reduced to such a state.

Now other sounds could be heard in the short pauses between the screams – rustles in the under-growth. The other dead witches were approaching us, drawn by Needle's anguish.

But then I heard something else. Thorne and I sniffed together, but this time it was not witch magic –

an attempt to discover a threat or gauge the strength of an enemy. It was something that any human would have recognized instantly; something that would fill a forester with fear.

I could smell smoke, burning wood, and I suddenly knew what our enemies had done.

'They've set fire to the dell!' Thorne cried.

I hoisted the sack up onto my shoulder. As I did so, a strong wind sprang up from the west, howling through the trees. They had conjured a gale and fire using dark magic, and the damp foliage would prove no impediment. Now the flames would sweep through the dell, consuming everything in their path.

Our enemies would not be forced to venture into the dell to find us, fighting any dead witches they encountered. They would be waiting in the clearing east of the dell; waiting for us to be driven out by the fire-storm.

CHAPTER 20
GRIMALKIN DOES NOT CRY

I anticipate a violent death
but will take many of my enemies with me!

What alternative did we have but to run east?
Already, even above the howling of the wind,
I could hear the crackle of burning wood, and dark
smoke gathered overhead, blocking out the light of the
moon.

'We will advance just ahead of the flames, then leave
the dell and cut down those in our path,' I told Thorne.

The words were easy to say, but to stay just ahead of
the conflagration was far from easy. For one thing the
smoke began to make our eyes water, forcing us into

fits of coughing. Secondly the fire was advancing very rapidly, leaping from tree to tree and from branch to branch with a crackling roar; it threatened to overtake us at any moment, and our slow jog soon became a fast sprint.

There were animals fleeing with us: a couple of hares and dozens of squealing rats, some of them with singed fur, some burning as they ran. I thought of poor Agnes. If the fire took her, at least her agony would be brief and that miserable existence in the dell as a weak dead witch would be over. But I knew that some inhabitants of the dell would survive by using their sharp talons to burrow into the leafy loam and down into the soft wet soil beneath. They had the means and the expertise gained by long years of survival here. It was not something that we could hope to do; we didn't have time.

The trees were thinning but we could see little through the smoke. Suddenly I sensed something approaching us from behind, and whirled to meet the new threat. It was a dead witch – the other strong one, clothes and hair aflame as she ran past, oblivious to us. She was screaming as she ran: the flames were consuming her and she realized that her time in the dell was over. Soon her soul would fall into the dark.

Where was the kretch? I wondered. No doubt it would be waiting somewhere ahead. As we left the trees, a witch attacked us from the left; this time a live one, from the vanguard of our enemies. Thorne cut her down without faltering, and we accelerated away from the danger.

Even above the whine of wind and roar of the fire I heard the eerie wail of the kretch somewhere behind us. Then it began to bay for our blood, a powerful rhythmical cry, as if a score of howling wolfhounds were on our trail.

'You are mine!' it called out, its voice booming through the night. *'You cannot escape! I will drink your blood and tear your flesh into strips! I will eat your hearts and gnaw the marrow from your shattered bones!'*

We were curving away south now; our path would take us east of Crow Wood. I thought of the lamia still in the tower. If only she'd had time to shape-shift to her winged form, she might have seen us and flown to our aid. But it was too soon for that. There was no hope of help from that source.

Then, as I ran, the warning lights once again flickered in the corners of my eyes. Would I have time enough lead Thorne to safety? But too soon the weakness was upon me again; I felt a fluttering in my chest and my breathing became shallow and ragged. I began to slow, and Thorne looked back at me in concern. I halted, hands on hips, aware of the irregular beating of my heart and the trembling in my legs. Now my whole body was shaking.

'No! No! Not now!' I shouted, forcing my body onwards, drawing upon my last reserves and every final shred of willpower. But it was useless. I managed to take only a dozen faltering steps before coming to a halt. Thorne paused and came back to stand by my side.

'You go on!' I cried. 'You can outrun them; I can't. It's the damage done by the poison.'

Thorne shook her head. 'I won't go without you!'

I lifted the sack off my shoulder and held it out to her. 'This is what matters. Take it and run. Keep it out of their hands at all costs.'

'I can't leave you to die.'

'You can and must,' I said, pushing the sack into her hands. 'Now go!'

I was resigned to dying here. I could do no more. I was spent.

Thorne swung the sack up onto her shoulder – but it was already too late.

There was a howl close behind us and the kretch padded into view.

The beast had changed again since the last time we'd faced it. There was something different about its eyes. They had regenerated since Thorne and I had pierced them with our blades, but not quite in the same way. There was a thin ridge of white bone above each one.

Moreover it was even larger. Its forearms seemed more muscular, the talons sharper and longer. There were more flecks of grey in its black fur too. Was it ageing already? Kretches usually had a short lifespan. Tibb, the last kretch the Malkins had created, had lived for only a few months.

In one fluid motion, Thorne drew a blade from a shoulder sheath and hurled it straight at the right eye of the beast. It was a good shot, exactly on target. But before the dagger struck, the ridge of bone moved. It flicked downwards, covering and protecting the eye so that the blade was deflected harmlessly away.

With the power inherited from its daemon father, the beast learned and improved itself all the time. Exploit a weakness, and the next time you encountered the creature, that weakness would be no more. Protected by armoured lids, its eyes were no longer easy targets for our blades.

I took a deep breath, tried to steady my trembling body and threw a blade at its throat, targeting a spot just below its left ear. The kretch seemed faster than ever: it brought up its left hand and swatted my blade aside. Again I staggered, and spots flashed within my eyes, bile rose in my throat. Then I saw what Thorne was attempting and cried out, 'No!'

To no avail. She was brave, but sometimes reckless too, and that latter quality was a dangerous fault that now became her undoing. She was the ten-year-old running at the bear again, a blade in her left hand. And it was that same blade, her first one; the one I had given her as we sat eating bear meat by the fire.

She was faster and far more deadly than the child who had stabbed the bear in the hind leg. However, the kretch was stronger and more dangerous than any bear which had ever walked this earth. And I was unable to repeat the throw that slew the beast before it killed her. I was on my knees, the world spinning, my mind falling into darkness.

The last thing I saw was the kretch opening its jaws wide and biting savagely into Thorne's left shoulder. She fought back, drawing another blade from a sheath with her right hand, stabbing it repeatedly into the beast's shoulder and head.

Then I knew no more.

* * *

How long I've lain here I know not, but I surmise that it is no more than an hour. I come to my knees slowly and am immediately sick, vomiting again and again, until only bile trickles from my mouth.

The kretch has gone. What has happened? Why didn't it kill me while I lay there, helpless? I stand groggily and begin to search for tracks. There was no evidence that witches have been here – just a muddy circle where the beast and Thorne fought, and then the prints of the kretch setting off northwards.

Has it carried Thorne off in its jaws . . . ?

I begin to follow the tracks. I am still unsteady on my feet but my strength is gradually returning and my breathing begins to slow to a more normal rhythm. I follow the trail of the kretch almost back to the edge of Witch Dell. The trees are still burning, but the magic is no more and the wind has changed direction. It is evident now that perhaps over half of Witch Dell will remain untouched by fire. But it has been cut in two by a broad black belt of burned trees.

Then I see something lying on the ground close to a blazing tree stump. It is a human body.

Is it that of the dead witch who fled the dell? I begin to move towards it, slowing with every step. I do not really want to reach it because, deep down, I already know whose corpse it is. The ground is churned to mud. Many witches have gathered here.

Moments later my worst fears are confirmed.

It is the body of Thorne.

There can be no doubt. No more room for hope.

She is lying on her back, stone dead. Her eyes are wide open and staring, an expression of horror and pain etched upon her face. The grass is wet with blood. Her hands have been mutilated. They have taken her thumb-bones, cut them from her body while she was still alive.

I kneel beside her and weep.

Grimalkin does not cry.

But I am crying now.

Time passes. How much I do not know.

I crouch before a fire, cooking meat on a spit. I turn

it slowly so that it is well done. Then I break it into two with my fingers and begin to eat it slowly.

There are two ways to make sure that a witch does not return from the dead. The first is to burn her; the second is to eat her heart.

So I have made doubly sure that Thorne's wishes are carried out. I have already burned her body. Now I am eating her heart. And still I am weeping.

When I have finished, I begin to speak aloud, my voice caught by the wind, spinning it away through the trees to the four corners of the earth.

'You were brave in life; be brave in death. Heed not the cackle of foolish witches. Your thumb-bones matter nought. They have taken them but cannot take away your courage; cannot negate what you were. For had you lived, you would have become the greatest witch assassin of the Malkin clan. You would have taken my place; surpassed my deeds; filled our enemies with dread.

'If reputation concerns you, then worry not. Who will be able to say, *We took her bones*? There will be nobody left to say it because none will live. I will kill them all. I will kill every last one.

'So rest in peace, Thorne, for what I say I will do.

'It will all come to pass.

'I am Grimalkin.'

CHAPTER
21
MY ONLY REMAINING ALLY

I am a hunter and also a blacksmith,
skilled in the art of forging weapons.
I could craft one especially for you;
the steel that would surely take your life.

At dawn I took stock of the situation and put aside my grief and anger. I needed to be cold and rational. I needed to think and plan.

Why had the kretch not killed me?

Maybe even as she died, Thorne had fought so fiercely, damaged it so badly, that it could not deal with us both? I said that to myself but knew that it was not true. I had been unconscious. It could have killed her, then dispatched me at its leisure.

No – the answer was clear. Even more important than my death was the retrieval of the sack containing the Fiend's head. That was its prime objective. It was created to kill me, but only as a means to an end – the reclaiming of the head and the resurrection of the Fiend. Thorne had been carrying it over her shoulder. Once the kretch had her in its jaws, it had the sack as well.

So it had taken the Fiend's head straight back to its creators. They had quickly cut away Thorne's thumb-bones and left her to die. Now they would be heading for the coast. They needed to return to Ireland to reunite head and body.

So what could I do? I had to follow. I had to try and stop them. But as I sat in the cold grey morning light, with my wrath set aside, I knew that I had little chance of success. My magic was used up, the resource gone. It would not be easy to restore it. My health was uncertain. I could suffer another bout of weakness at any time. And I was alone. Alone against so many.

I needed help, but who could I turn to now? The
answer came immediately:

Alice Deane.

She was the only remaining ally I could rely on.
Recently all who had tried to help me had died. I had
sought out Agnes and Thorne, and both had died as a
result. So many had died, including Wynde, the lamia,
and the knight whom I had manipulated to serve
my cause. Could I do it again, thus placing Alice in
danger? Was I right to ask another friend to risk her
life?

Grimalkin should not ask such questions. To think
like that was to show weakness. I must act and not
think too much about the possible consequences.

But I would not seek the help of Thomas Ward or
John Gregory. The apprentice was too valuable to risk.
He might be the means of finally destroying the Fiend.
No, I could not take a chance with his life. Once the
head was retrieved and the kretch dead, I would escort
him to Malkin Tower. The sooner the better.

As for the Spook, he was past his best, and in any

case had too many scruples. He would not have the stomach for what I must do. So I would simply ask Alice. Two witches together – that would be best. She might be willing to lend me some of her strength.

I pulled my mirror from its sheath and prepared to make contact with her. Three times I tried, but I could not reach her. Even that small magic was beyond me. I was drained and needed replenishing.

I would have to go to her. I would travel to Chipenden, where the Spook was starting to rebuild his house.

I followed the tracks of my enemies, passing north of Pendle and heading towards the Ribble Valley. The tracks went west then, but did not cross the ford; they kept south of the river. That meant they were not heading for Sunderland Point. They would go to Liverpool and seize a boat there.

Moving as fast as I was able, I reluctantly left their trail and crossed the Ribble, heading northwest. I had to go to Chipenden first. It would mean losing perhaps half a day, but I could still catch the witches before they sailed.

I avoided the village itself and began to climb the lane to the boundary of the Spook's property. Once I would not have risked entering the garden. But Alice had told me that the boggart that had once guarded it was gone, its pact with John Gregory ended when the house burned and the roof collapsed.

Even so, I entered the trees of the western garden slowly and cautiously. In the distance I could see the Spook's house. As I drew nearer, I also saw trestle tables and huge planks and other building materials. Out of sight, someone was sawing wood. The roof had already been replaced, and a thin spiral of smoke was rising from a chimneypot. Then suddenly I heard distant voices; voices that I recognized.

Although my magic had gone, some witch skills are innate – especially that of sniffing. It was Alice and Tom Ward, the apprentice. The Spook wasn't with them. No doubt he was warming his old bones close to the fire.

So I crept closer and crouched behind the trunk of a large tree.

'It just ain't right, Tom,' I heard Alice say. 'Nothing's changed. No matter what I do, Old Gregory will never trust me. Why can't I come with you? Try talking to him again.'

'I'll do my best,' Tom replied, 'but you know how stubborn he can be. He wants to set off first thing tomorrow, but we'll probably only be away for a few days, Alice. You'll be comfortable here.'

'I'm probably better off staying here anyway!' Alice retorted. 'You two had best go and sort through them mouldy old books. Anyway, you get back to the house, Tom. I'm going for a walk to think things through. Feel better for a walk, I will.'

'Don't be like that, Alice. It's not my fault and you know it.'

But Alice wouldn't listen and began to stroll in my direction, and after a moment Tom bowed his head and walked back towards the house. As she passed me, Alice glanced in my direction. It was a shock to see her white hair – the result of being snatched away into the dark and tormented by the Fiend and his servants. She smiled, then walked on, leaving the garden and crossing the field towards the lane. She had sniffed out my presence and had worked out the situation – she knew that I didn't want to be seen by Tom.

I followed her down into the lane, where she moved under the shadow of some trees and waited for me. Before leaving Ireland, she had contacted me to tell me of her experiences when she'd been taken into the dark. I couldn't get used to the sight of her white hair.

Her eyes widened as I approached. 'Where's the Fiend's head?' she demanded.

'Our enemies have it, Alice. They seized it yesterday, and they're now taking it to the coast – to Liverpool, I think. I need your help!'

Alice looked afraid – and with good reason. If the Fiend's supporters succeeded in reuniting the head with the body, the Fiend would walk the earth once more. Tom and Alice no longer had the blood jar as a means of defence. His first act would be to seize them and drag them off into the dark, and then they'd face an eternity of torment.

'What sort of help? What can I do?'

'My magic's gone, Alice, all used up.'

'Magic ain't everything,' Alice said. 'You're Grimalkin. You can use your blades. Hunt 'em down one by one. What's wrong with you? Never heard you talk like this. What am I supposed to do?'

'My blades won't be enough, Alice. There are too many of them. I need my own magic to deflect theirs, and to be able to cloak myself and retain an element of surprise. Then there's the kretch – it was specially made to kill me and take back the head. It's formidable. It's already killed one of the lamias left to guard Malkin Tower. Its claws are coated with a deadly poison. It hurt me badly, Alice; now I am plagued by bouts of weakness.'

'My aunt, Agnes Sowerbutts, could help. Some wouldn't agree, though I reckon she's the best healer in Pendle.'

'She tried, Alice. She pulled me back from the brink

of death, but I'm permanently damaged. You can't believe how bad things have been. Agnes is dead. They killed her. They killed Thorne too, and took her thumb-bones while she was still alive and—'

I was going to say more about how brave Thorne had been and how she'd saved me after I'd been poisoned, but I had to stop, choked with emotion.

As Alice took in the full import of what I was saying, her eyes widened in horror.

'So I need some of your magic, Alice. You've plenty. Just transfer some to me.'

'No!' Alice cried, clenching her fists at her side. 'I won't do it. Build up your own magic again – you can do it.'

What Alice meant was that I should kill, take the thumb-bones of my victims and carry out the necessary rituals. Yes, it could be done, but there wasn't time.

'Within a day they will have sailed for Ireland with the Fiend's head. There simply isn't time to replenish my magic using the normal methods. Give me some of *your* power, Alice. Heal me as well. You've more power than you need. You can do it.'

Alice was a special kind of witch – a type rarely found. Although she didn't practise the rituals of blood, bone or familiar magic, she had a power within her. Tremendous innate power that was part of her being; part of being Alice.

'I can't touch it – you know that!' Alice retorted. 'Use the dark and you end up being part of the dark. Don't want that, do I?'

'You've used it before,' I accused her.

'That's true enough. I did so in Ireland to save Tom, so I can't risk using it again now.'

'You have to take the risk. Otherwise the Fiend will come for you – and soon. How long will it take them to dig him up from the pit and join the head to the body? Even counting the sea voyage and the journey across Ireland to Kerry, he could well come for you within the week. Tom too! That's how long you've got, Alice, if you don't help me now.'

Alice was quiet for a long time; when she spoke, her

voice was little more than a whisper. 'All right, I'll come with you. We'll follow 'em and see what's what, but I ain't promising anything. Wait here – I'll just go and tell Tom.'

'No, that would be a mistake. We don't want to lead him into danger; nor that master of his. Besides, they're off somewhere tomorrow. I overheard your conversation in the garden. They'll be away for a few days and it'll all be over before they get back.'

'They're going east to the County border,' Alice replied. 'Old Gregory's heard of a collection of books about the dark. He's hoping to get his hands on some to restock his library. You're right. Let's leave Tom and Old Gregory out of it.'

So, without further words, we set off in a westerly direction. Within hours we had picked up the trail of our enemies and were heading towards the coast.

CHAPTER 22

A MALEVOLENT WITCH

*Alice Deane has the potential to become
the most powerful witch who has ever lived.*

We followed our enemies with great caution, gradually overhauling them; by the time we sniffed out that they'd made camp for the night, we were only two miles behind.

We settled down in a grove of trees and watched their campfires spark into life like fireflies. We were close and already in danger. We were able to sniff them out, but they could do likewise. They might well send some of their party back to deal with us.

'Alice, you need to use some of your magic now to

cloak us. The kretch was able to find me despite my best efforts to hide myself, so the spell needs to be as strong as you can make it!'

Alice nodded, then settled down with her back against a tree trunk, closed her eyes and began to mutter to herself. The moon was out, casting dappled shadows on the ground. By its light I studied Alice's face. Even without taking into account her white hair, her face looked older. It was still that of a girl, but now it had a maturity that belied her years. She had seen too much.

When she opened her eyes, I was momentarily shocked. They were still youthful and pretty, but it was as if some ancient, powerful being stared out at me; something hardly human that had dwelt on earth since time began. It only lasted for a second, and disappeared as she began to smile, but I shivered all the same.

'It's done,' she said. 'They can't find us now.'

'Next you must try to heal me,' I told her. 'Do it now. Heal me first, then give me some of your magic.'

The smile slipped from her face. 'Ain't sure if I can do it,' she responded.

To give me some of her magic was feasible. Pendle witches sometimes did it – though grudgingly; they were like money-lenders, expecting it to be returned threefold at a later date. But it might well be that Alice would be unable to heal me. Agnes had failed, and healing had been her speciality. Sometimes sheer power simply wasn't enough. But, as it turned out, Alice wasn't actually doubting her ability; she was afraid of the consequences.

'It's really dark magic and it could cost me too much,' she said, and now it was her turn to shiver. 'I could end up being a fully malevolent witch. That's why Old Gregory don't trust me. He's always believed that's the way I'll turn out.'

I shrugged. 'Being a malevolent witch isn't that bad, Alice. It's what I am. You'd be no worse than me. You can't fight your own nature. Maybe it's what you were always born to be.'

'There are worse witches than you, Grimalkin. You've a code of honour. You don't kill for fun, but slay those who deserve to die. You love hunting strong enemies who put up a good fight, but you don't trample on the weak. There are some witches who do; some witches who glory in power and in hurting others. I don't want to end up like them. I'm afraid that in using the power I've been given, that's exactly how I will end up. Best not forget who I am – the daughter of the Fiend!'

'You'll always be what you were destined to be, Alice. Like Tom Ward, you have a path to follow, and you must take the necessary steps or always be less than you could be. Now heal me and give me some of your power. Please do it – otherwise the Fiend will walk the earth once more. He will come for you and then for Tom.'

Alice shivered, but then she nodded. 'I've no choice, have I? Kneel facing the north,' she commanded, 'and I'll do what I can.'

I obeyed, falling to my knees and facing north – the direction that was most conducive to both the healing and the transfer of power.

Alice placed her hands on my forehead. 'First I'll try

to heal you,' she said, her voice hardly more than a whisper.

I don't know what I expected to happen. With a healer like Agnes Sowerbutts, the use of herbs and plant extracts was as important as the words and ritual. I knew that Alice administered such medicines herself and carried them in a leather pouch, but now she was using nothing more than her hands on my head. She didn't even chant a spell.

'It's really difficult,' she said after a while. 'The poison lies deep within. It's oozed into every part of your body. In places the damage is subtle; in others obvious and severe. I'm going to have to use more magic, but I'm scared of hurting you. There's even a risk that the process could kill you,' she warned.

'Don't let that concern you,' I answered. 'I would rather be dead than less than what I was.'

'That's your choice. But if you're dead, who'll retrieve the Fiend's head?'

'I cannot retrieve it in my present state, so what's the difference?' I said. 'If I die, go and get Thomas Ward.

Work together. Only you two will stand any chance against our enemies.'

I felt a slight tremor in Alice's fingers, and then she pressed them into my skull and the world spun about me. My breathing gradually became faster, as did my heartbeat. I began to tremble all over. There were sharp pains in my stomach and chest, as if some invisible being were plunging a needle into my flesh over and over again.

Quickly the process reached a crisis. My heart was now beating so fast that the individual pulses of blood merged and it seemed to be vibrating continuously. I felt as if I were dying, but then a surge of warmth flowed out of Alice's fingertips and I fell forward on to my face and momentarily lost consciousness.

I felt myself being pulled back up into a kneeling position, and opened my eyes.

'How do you feel?' Alice asked.

'Weak,' I said, aware that my heart was now beating slowly and steadily again. 'Did you succeed?'

'Yes, I'm certain of it.' Alice gave a proud smile. 'The last traces of the poison and its effects upon your body are gone.'

What she had done was more than impressive – it was astounding. Where Agnes, with all her skill and knowledge, had failed to find me a permanent cure, Alice had succeeded. She was still a girl, but how formidable would she be as a woman and a fully-fledged witch? What better ally could I have on my side?

'I thank you for that, Alice. Now lend me the magical power I need – the power to retrieve the Fiend's head and deal with our enemies.'

Once more Alice laid her hand upon me. For a moment she hesitated and I sensed her reluctance: I glared at her angrily. Then, with a sharp intake of breath, she began to chant the spell of transference; within seconds a tingle started at my head and moved down my neck towards my heart and then to my extremities. She was giving me some of her magic – a lot of it. It was going straight into my body. I wouldn't need to draw it from my necklace; it would be available the moment I willed it. The process went on for a long time. And it felt right.

I was filled with new hope. Finally I believed that I would succeed.

At first light we picked up the trail of our enemies again; it was now apparent that they were not making for Liverpool after all. Their route led more directly westwards. They were heading straight for the sea, many miles north of that town.

'Don't want to draw unwelcome attention to themselves, do they?' Alice said. 'That many witches and a kretch – they're best kept out of sight. Liverpool's a sea port that does lots of trade. Got their own militia, they have, to look after the interests of all those rich merchants. Those part-time soldier boys wouldn't take kindly to a bunch of witches strolling into town. So they'll be looking for somewhere quieter. One of the villages further north, maybe. Then they'll send a couple of witches into Liverpool to terrorize a captain and crew.'

'What if they just send those couple of witches straight back to Ireland with the head? In that case they'd only need a small fishing boat,' I said.

'Would you follow 'em?' asked Alice.

'I would if I had to,' I replied. 'Let's hope it doesn't come to that.'

As it turned out, we were both proved wrong. We were moving across mossy flat land now and, despite Alice's cloaking magic, we could still be seen against the skyline, so we had dropped back another mile or so.

But then, in the distance, we saw the ship lying at anchor. She was large, with three masts, and her sails were already unfurled. The tide would be changing to ebb and she was ready for her voyage. Our enemies had prepared everything in advance. They had chartered a ship and must have sent word by mirror to other witches already waiting on board.

We began to run, but when we reached the shore, we could see the kretch and a couple of witches some distance away on the sands, staring at the ship – which was already beginning to turn away, the wind filling her sails. The majority of our enemies were on board, and they had the Fiend's head in their possession. We had arrived too late.

'I have to follow. We need a boat of our own.' I pointed towards a village in the distance. 'That's Formby – there will be fishermen there.'

Alice shook her head. 'She's a big ship, that, with lots of sails. She would reach Ireland long before any fishing boat. They'll have prepared everything, they will. Coaches with fast teams of horses will be ready to take them to the southwest. It'll be over long before you can reach Kenmare.'

In my mind's eye I saw the village of Kenmare once more: the circle of standing stones and, at its centre, the huge boulder and the earth hiding the flat stone beneath which the Fiend's body was impaled upon silver spears. I saw my enemies digging it up, freeing it and then reuniting it with the head. I saw the fury in that monster's bestial face and his lust for revenge. I had borne his child so he couldn't come for me unless I allowed it. But Alice and Tom would be his first victims, and with Tom's death my last chance of destroying him for ever would be gone. Eventually I too would die, and even a dead witch cannot exist within the dell for ever. Inevitably I would go to the dark, and the Fiend would be waiting for me – time was nothing to an immortal.

'You've got to use your magic, Alice. We can't just let them escape or it's over for all of us – you, me, Tom and John Gregory. Surely you can do something?'

'There is a way, but it'll cost me again!' Alice said, her voice full of bitterness. 'What choice do I have now? Everything's against me. It's as if all this was meant to happen long in advance. I ain't got no choice but to go along with it!'

She raised her arms and pointed up into the sky; then she began to chant. At first it was hardly more than a sing-song under her breath, but as she began to spin, her voice grew steadily louder.

There had been a wind blowing from the south-east filling the ship's sails, but now that stopped very suddenly. I watched the sails become limp.

Was that what Alice Deane was trying to accomplish? To use her magic to becalm the ship and prevent it from sailing for Ireland? If so, how long could she hope to maintain such a situation?

'What are you trying to do, Alice?' I demanded. There had to be a better way of dealing with our enemies.

But Alice did not reply; she looked rapt, deep in a magical trance, gathering her power.

I need not have concerned myself because, within seconds, everything changed dramatically. The wind sprang up again, but this time from a different direction – from the west, from the sea, driving straight into our faces. It lifted clouds of sand up off the beach and drove spray towards me, stinging my face – which I covered with my hands, peering through my fingers.

I saw the witches and the kretch turn away and cower down on the sands with their backs to the waves; they were much closer to the sea, and the salt spray would be burning them. Salt water is deadly to witches, and those on board the ship would be wearing protective hoods and gloves – maybe knitted face-masks too – and cowering down in the hold. Despite the frantic efforts of the crew, the ship was now turning in the water. Faster and faster she came about, and the surging waves began to move her towards the shore.

Alice was still chanting and spinning, her voice almost lost in the shrill shrieks of the wind. Dark clouds raced in from the sea and the gale drove the ship before it relentlessly. There was no way the crew could turn her round. Soon she would run aground.

But for the witches there was even worse to come.

Forked lighting ripped the sky apart to the west, and within less than a second there came an answering deep rumble of thunder, like the growl of a huge vengeful beast. The second flash of lightning came at the same time as the thunderclap. The third lit the whole sky and struck the central mast of the ship, which instantly ignited. Suddenly the whole sail was on fire, and then, moments later, the second and third sails were alight. We could hear the screams and shouts of those on board, carried to us by the wind.

Which would be first? Would the boat run aground, or would it burn? Whatever happened, it was no place for witches. Either they would burn or they would be immersed in salt water.

Then I saw figures climbing down the rope ladder to the two small boats lashed to the ship's stern. One witch shrieked as she fell into the waves. Thrashing about desperately, she sank within seconds. But others were managing to clamber into the boats. Some of them might survive.

I glanced at Alice and saw the exultation in her face. She was enjoying this; relishing her power. And why shouldn't she? This was a formidable display of magic. Even after weeks of preparation the whole Malkin coven would be hard pressed to match this spontaneous display of raw magical power.

Now was the best time to attack. I should cut them down as they walked up the beach – the kretch too if it got in my way. But then Alice stopped spinning and fell to the ground. I quickly ran forward and knelt beside her.

For one terrible moment I thought that her spirit had fled her body. It is possible for a witch to over-extend herself, using so much of her power that her body can no longer function. Although Alice was hardly breathing and had exhausted herself to the point of death, she was somehow clinging onto life. I let out a sigh of relief.

The immediate crisis was over. For now our enemies were going nowhere far. So I picked Alice up, threw her over my shoulder and retreated from the shore.

I took refuge in an abandoned farmhouse. There were only three walls standing, but it provided shelter from the chill westerly wind. The roof would provide no protection from the rain; all that remained of it was the wooden supports, a ribcage above which a gibbous moon glinted through the patchwork of fast-moving clouds.

If our enemies still had the Fiend's head, I would

take it from them later. Perhaps it had sunk to the bottom of the sea. At least that would put it beyond the reach of witches. But no doubt in time they would get someone to dive and retrieve it for them. For now, however, the immediate danger was over: I could deal with my enemies at my leisure, slaying them one by one. I shivered with pleasure. I had waited a long time for this and I intended to savour each succulent moment of my revenge.

I had decided to attend to Alice and seek them out later, after dark. She opened her eyes and looked up at me, then tried to sit up. The effort was too much for her, and I rested my hand on her shoulder in reassurance. Her eyes closed.

'Sleep,' I commanded her softly. 'You are exhausted.'

She resisted and tried in vain to open her eyes again; after a few moments the rhythm of her breathing told me that she had fallen into a deep sleep. It was true that using such powerful magic had exhausted her, but I had also given her something to ensure that she would sleep until dawn at least. I had used an infusion of two herbs. She had taken three sips, that was all, but it was enough for my purposes.

I looked at her hair and smiled. It was dark at the roots. Soon it would grow out as black as it was before. But would her mind heal as quickly? I doubted it. Few had suffered as much as Alice at the hands of the Fiend.

The survivors of the shipwreck had gathered in a wood about three miles to the south of us. I had been close to them already without being detected and had sniffed out their situation. Now I carried out one final reconnaissance, this time using powerful magic to cloak myself. I moved in. In all, about thirty remained; but, to my delight, I saw that eight of the witches were suffering from the effects of salt water, two so badly contaminated that they were sure to die. I sniffed repeatedly to learn as much as possible about their situation. It was wonderful to sense the general feeling of gloom and desperation. Most of them were clearly terrified; after all, they had let down their lord, the Fiend. They feared his wrath.

Using their magic, they had already discovered the means by which their ship had been destroyed and were afraid of Alice and the power she had wielded. But they feared me too.

Only the mage and the kretch were still confident of their ability to defeat me. But, most important of all, I learned that the Fiend's head was still in their possession. The mage, Bowker, was carrying it. This was my priority.

I had drugged Alice because I wanted to protect her; if she was with me there was a danger that she might get hurt. But I also wanted to be the one to wreak revenge on my enemies. Besides, I prefer to work alone.

CHAPTER
23
OH, MR WOLF!

Are you my enemy? Are you strong, with speed and
agility and the training of a warrior?
It matters nought to me. Run now!
Run fast into the forest!
I'll give you a few moments' start – an hour if you wish.
But you will never be fast enough.
I'll catch and kill you before long.

Before I leave the sleeping Alice, I think of poor
Thorne again, and grief knots my stomach. But I
counter that by going over the happy times we shared
and remember the way she grew in strength and skill,
becoming more than I had ever hoped for her. Finally,

before I put my memories of Thorne aside, my mind returns to a question she once asked me:

Have you ever taken the thumb-bones of your enemies while they were still alive?

I refused to give her an answer. Whether I have done so or not is my business and not the concern of others. But it suits me if my enemies think that I do. This is why I carve the image of my scissors on trees to warn them off.

Now I am ready – ready to kill; ready to kill them all. I have become the mother of death. She trots at my heels, hanging onto my skirt, giggling with glee, leaving wet footprints of red blood on the green grass. Can you hear her laughter? Listen for it in the cries of the carrion crows who will feast on the flesh of my victims.

I stand at the edge of the wood. As a result of the healing and the magic that Alice gave me, I am strong; perhaps stronger than ever before. I am so well cloaked that my enemies are totally unaware of my presence. The prospect of combat excites me and I am more than ready to fight and kill. They expect an attack but know not the precise moment when it will strike or from which direction. Thus I retain some element of surprise.

My blades are ready in their scabbards; so are my scissors. Once I have slain my enemies, I will take their thumb-bones. Thus I will increase my store of magic even further. I must retrieve the Fiend's head and keep it safe from those who covet it. So I need all the magic I can get. I must also return to Alice that which she gave me. No doubt one day she will have need of it.

I attack. I am fast, so very fast. Never have I been faster!

One runs at me from the left. I draw and flick the blade, all in one fluid movement. It catches the witch in the throat and she falls heavily – the first of my enemies to die.

Where is the kretch?

I sniff, and immediately know that it is far below me, to the left. There are many enemies between us. No matter. I will kill them first. My long blade is in my left hand now. I cut and kill a witch who runs straight at me. But now they have all sniffed me out. They are converging, anticipating my progress down through the trees. So I begin to slow down, changing direction slightly to draw them after me.

At last I come to a halt in a small clearing and await their attack. They encircle me and close in rapidly, moving towards me through the trees. They are eager to reach me. Tighter and tighter the circle becomes, and I hear feet drumming on the ground, getting louder and louder. Within seconds the first of them will burst out of the cover of the trees, and into the circular clearing where I stand.

I am ready.

This is the killing ground.

And far beyond the circle of blades, the kretch is still waiting, the mage at its side.

Oh, Mr Wolf! Soon it will be your turn!

The bravest witches come in hard and fast. They die first. I whirl and cut and spin, slicing and stabbing until the air is filled with the shrieks, curses and screams of my enemies; until the grass is slick with their blood.

Others press in behind them: Lisa Dugdale, Jenny Croston and Maggie Lunt. These are the three from Pendle who have lashed blades to long sticks. They seek to jab and stab from a distance – with less risk to themselves. These are the ones who cut and slew Wynde, the lamia, when she lay helpless with a broken wing in the jaws of the kretch; these are the cowards who tried to pierce the armour of the knight when he was down and at their mercy. So I find it satisfying to pay them back in kind.

So these I maim rather than kill outright. They limp away, hoping to reach safety. I will hunt them down afterwards. It will be something to savour.

My enemies fall back and begin to flee. Now there is only the mage and the kretch to deal with. Bowker steps forward, the leather sack on his shoulder, and points the small rodent skull at my head. He chants, and something invisible but deadly surges towards me; I hear a ringing in my ears.

I stagger and almost fall, and suddenly I am weak and defenceless. Bowker laughs and comes towards me, the weapon still pointing at my head, a blade readied in his other hand.

'It was I who took the bones of the girl, Grimalkin! And now I will take yours!' he cries.

He is less than ten steps away when I rally, drawing upon the magic that Alice has given me. It is stronger than the weapon he has used against me; stronger than anything he has at his disposal. I show my teeth, draw a dagger from its sheath and hurl it towards him. It buries itself in his leg and he drops to one knee. Seeing the death in my eyes, he turns and flees, limping towards the trees, leaving a trail of blood on the grass. He still has the Fiend's head but will not get far. Soon he will be mine.

'Mr Wolf!' I cry. 'Now it is your turn! I am here! I am Grimalkin! Now we fight to the death!'

The kretch bounds towards me, forelimbs out-stretched, eager to rend the flesh from my bones. It rears up, towering over me, and slashes at me with its talons.

I whirl and spin, avoiding their sharp poisonous tips, and the hilt of my blade smashes hard into its mouth, making of it a bloody ruin. It reminds me of what I did to the Fiend, and I smile.

Oh, Mr Wolf! What big teeth you had!

I laugh as it shakes its head and the shattered teeth fall from its mouth. Some of them are red with blood, and it is enraged as I spring away; now it is snarling and spinning like a mad dog trying to catch its elusive tail. But it is slow, so very slow, and I am lithe and nimble. We dance together; the dance of death that it promised me.

Oh, Mr Wolf! What big eyes you had!

My words are true because my blades have taken them both, stabbing faster than a blink, straight in under the bone shields. Now the kretch is blind again. This time it will not be given the chance to recover. This time only death awaits it.

I stab and cut as if in a frenzy. But each blow is meas-

ured; each slicing of its flesh calculated and precise –
until it is weak and the ground is soaked in its blood.

Oh, Mr Wolf! What a big heart you had!

Now I hold the heart of the kretch in my hands. At
first it still beats, but soon it is still and begins to cool.
I cut it into tiny pieces and scatter the bloody fragments on the ground. Finally I dismember the body
and scatter it to the wind.

The crows will feast well.

But its thumb-bones I keep. Later they will join the
others that I wear around my neck.

CHAPTER
24
THE HUNT

My favourite weapon is the long blade:
I use it for fighting at close quarters.
Think you can beat me?
It is already buried in your heart!

The kretch is dead, and now I keep my promise:
the ones who slew Thorne must all die too.
So I begin the hunt.
I break the back of Lisa Dugdale.
I hang her from an oak by her toes;
I drain her blood;
I take her bones.
I drown Jenny Croston in a deep cold pond.

I hold her head underwater while her limbs thrash;
I drain her blood;
I take her bones.
Maggie Lunt begs like a frightened child.
I kill her quickly; my knife splits her heart;
I drain her blood;
I take her bones.
Finally I catch and slay Bowker, the mage;
I take his bones;
I drain his blood.
Thus Thorne is avenged –
For who is left to say:
'We took her bones'?
None, because all are dead,
And I took theirs.
I am Grimalkin.

CHAPTER
25
A SORRY SIGHT INDEED

I sense your threat!
How strong are you?
Are you worth my time?
Shall I look for you in my mirror!

I sit cross-legged, sheltering by a hawthorn hedge, and remove the Fiend's head from the leather sack. I place it on the grass before me.

It is a sorry sight indeed, and I smile. They have not attempted to unpick the stitches from his remaining eye, but the green apple and rose thorns have been plucked from his mouth. The head groans, showing the yellow stumps of teeth.

'I win again!' I cry. 'Despite all that your followers attempted, you are still in my power. The kretch and your servants are all dead!'

The Fiend does not reply. Even when I prod the lid of the stitched eye hard with a stick, it does not flicker. The head is cold, still and silent, almost as if the Fiend has deserted it and returned to the dark. But that cannot be because he is trapped within it.

He does not reply because, for now, he is defeated. I have won, his followers are slain, and he cannot bear to confront the victor. I have damaged him badly and I feel deeply satisfied.

I no longer have an apple or thorns at my disposal; instead I use a tangle of nettles and hawthorn twigs, ramming them into the Fiend's mouth with considerable force. Then, with a smile of triumph, I thrust the head back into the sack.

This stage of our battle against the Fiend's servants has ended successfully. So now it is vital that Tom Ward travels to Malkin Tower to study what his mother has bequeathed to him. I will offer him all the help he needs so that he can discover the means by which we can finally destroy the Fiend!

But the closer we come to achieving that aim, the greater the danger will become. No doubt soon there will be another threat.

A witch cannot scry her own death but she can do it for another. Recently I have foreseen a new threat to Alice. The mirror went dark so it allows a little hope. But I am deeply concerned. Four of us: Thomas Ward, John Gregory, Alice and I are bound together in this enterprise.

I fear that not all of us will survive.